GOOD BLOOD,
BAD BLOOD

Satisfied that his movement was not noticed, Crane stepped quickly through the door of the *jacal*.

Tito watched him disappear inside. "Bastard!" he hissed.

Neville nodded. Then from within the *jacal* came what they both feared most—a shrill, feminine scream, quavering with loathing and fury. The words carried clearly to them:

"You filthy son of a bitch!"

Every head in the enclosure jerked toward the *jacal*. Tito stiffened ironhard beside Neville.

"No waiting now, compañero!"

He leaped into the clear, drawing his holstered gun and the spare in his belt, and Neville plunged after him, clutching his rifle. . . .

COMPAÑEROS

Tom W. Blackburn

A DELL BOOK

Published by
Dell Publishing Co., Inc.
1 Dag Hammarskjold Plaza
New York, New York 10017

Copyright © 1978 by Thomas Wakefield Blackburn

Dell ® TM 681510, Dell Publishing Co., Inc.

ISBN: 0-440-11013-0

Printed in the United States of America
First printing—February 1978

COMPAÑEROS

Chapter 1

The Corona house, now much enlarged, had originally been built on the site of Spencer Stanton's first camp on the grant of which he was to become master. More properly, it was the site of the crude brush *jacal* 'Mana Stanton and her Ute friends had built to shelter him while he lay insensible with a would-be murderer's bullet in his back. As a result it had been situated with Indianlike attention to defense and avoidance of surprise attack.

It lay out on a gently rolling plain of open grass some miles to the east of the abrupt front range of the snowcapped Sangre de Cristos. The view was unobstructed for a great distance in all directions. A small cold stream of sweet water from the mountains ran past and no approach could be made within several miles except across the open vastness surrounding it.

In time, as the ranch prospered and the house grew, an adobe village rose from the sod near the stock corrals half a mile down the creek. There were now more than a dozen of the neatly whitewashed little adobes. Serving them was a sizeable ranch store and a small chapel beneath its cross.

Some close-in grass had been reluctantly turned for garden plots and the field crop necessary to support such an establishment in so remote a place. Trees had been planted where nature had put none. A well-pruned orchard, fenced off by whitewashed rails against stock and game alike, lay back of the main house. The foreyard was well shaded by cottonwoods towering above the second-story eaves and a double row flanked the lane leading down to the village.

The house, with block walls of native red sandstone as much as thirty inches thick, had the timeless permanence and formidable strength of this New Mexico high country itself. The thick, handmade tiles of its roofing sometimes caught the sun for miles across the eastward grass. It was at once a citadel and a monument.

Spencer Stanton had built it over the years for his wife, but it was his mark that was upon it. It was mortared with his ambitions and his dreams. 'Mana Stanton's was a gentler nature. Her influence was within, notable in the gracious richness of the furnishings, the effortless, unstinting hospitality at any hour of the day or night, and the courteous, soft-spoken voices of the children and the household staff when they were in her presence.

In a very real sense the massive house was the essence of the Corona, a visible symbol of that greater entity of unbroken land that stretched beyond the horizon in every direction. It was equally a symbol of the dedication and determination of those who had in a few short years built so much from a recorded sheet of ancient parchment describing the grant of a forgotten king at the time of Spanish colonization.

The two men pulled up at about a mile's distance, absently letting their two trailing packhorses nuzzle the grass cropped down fetlock-high this close to headquarters. They were young, both rather handsome in a dark southern way, and obviously not of the high country. Their eyes were clear, level, with the slightly sardonic surety of self-knowledge that is sometimes bred into an aristocratic line. There could be no doubt of their relationship. They were brothers.

Both wore soft-brimmed campaign hats, each raked at an angle to suit its wearer's personality. Each otherwise dressed as suited him but their clothing was well-cut and expensive in quality. Boot leather and belts were brightly polished beneath the dust now overlaying them. Their horses were sleek. If they had come far it had been in no haste. Nevertheless, they were armed and there was purpose about them.

The older and also the slightly taller had lost his right hand an inch or two above the wrist. It was replaced by a sharp, gleaming steel hook laced snugly and unobtrusively to the stump. The hook seemed to incorporate some kind of a gripping device actuated by forearm muscle.

The injury had not been recent. The man was too unconscious of the handicap. He pushed his hat back with the hook and shook his head wryly at the formidable house and sprawling establishment ahead.

"Christ, Blair, did you think it would turn out to be something like this?"

"Not by a damned sight," the younger man answered with his own awe. "The old man's really got himself a layout, hasn't he?"

"Probably complete to a throne room and a standing army. It may take more doing than we figured."

"Well, now's the time to back out. Another mile and it'll be too late."

"Back out, better than two thousand miles from home? After Antietam and Shiloh—all we have coming?" The speaker clicked the gripping device on the hook defiantly. "We'll do her, boy. Just as we planned. Go in easy. Real easy. Till we see where we are and just what we're up against. All right?"

"Whatever you say. Like always, J. Far as I'm concerned this is something. Really something. It ought to be worth a little sweat."

"Don't let it show. Follow my lead. Unless I miss my guess, there'll be linen on the table at supper tonight."

The man with the hook grinned. He tugged down his hat and took up his reins. Packhorses trailing, they rode on.

The Corona headquarters lay tranquil as they continued their approach. The shrill voices of children at play

came from the adobes of the village. Dogs barked. Dust
rose over loose stock in the corrals. There seemed little
human curiosity. But there was wariness. Perhaps only
a natural characteristic of the place and people.

A man in a Mexican hat stooped through the rails of
one of the corrals with the ease of long practice. He
straightened and studied the strangers. Coming to some
conclusion, he moved unhurriedly to a saddled horse
tethered to the rails and swung up. There was a rifle
sheathed beneath his right stirrup leathers. He rode at
an ambling jog up the lane toward the main house, timing his pace to that of the two riders coming in from the
eastward grass. If his errand involved them it did not
show.

Two more men came out of the store. They took
mounts at the rack there in the same style and direction.
They also were armed.

A fourth man emerged from the orchard. He approached the house from the rear, riding down along
the creek-bank without haste. He appeared to have
been varmint-hunting among the fruit trees or had some
other need for a ready weapon. A rifle was cradled under his free arm.

"Welcoming committee," the younger of the two
strangers growled.

"Mexican hospitality," his brother agreed. "Not quite
like they told it out on the Trail. Just to make sure—"

Deftly using his hook, he unfastened his gunbelt. Re-
pinning it, he hung it from his saddlehorn. The younger
brother did likewise. They shortened the leads on their
packhorses, drawing their heads up abreast the flanks of
their mounts for better control as they had learned to do
on long cavalry patrols when it seemed likely an uncertain confrontation was imminent.

They rode in this fashion into the foreyard of the big
house and pulled up before the broad veranda running
across the front of the central portion of the imposing
building. The man from the orchard came around from
the rear and stopped at the corner of the house, his rifle

resting easily across his thighs. Surprisingly in this distant place, he was a black. He was hatless, apparently habitually so, and the easy set of his body warned of enormous physical strength. His expression told the newcomers nothing.

The three riders from the adobe village down the creek halted a similar distance away. Their arms were at hand but the weapons remained sheathed. Their faces under their big hats were dark mahogany and as inscrutable as that of the black man. No one spoke.

The silence held for a long moment. Then the great, thick-planked main door of the house opened. Two men emerged. One was quite young, about twenty, but a good deal of time and experience had left their stamp upon him. He moved with extraordinarily quick and light-footed grace. The indefinable aura of command, which during the war had made, in a few brief weeks, seasoned officers out of otherwise raw recruits, clung to him.

The other was a plainer man, twice the age of the first, harder used and with a commoner look. Both were hard of body, leaned by the saddle, deeply tanned by the high-country sun, and with the chill of the westward mountains in their set, noncommittal expressions. Neither offered greeting or challenge.

The stranger with the hook shifted uncomfortably in his saddle.

"This the Stanton place?" he asked.

"It is," the younger man on the veranda agreed. "I'm Tito Stanton. This is Jaime Henry, our *segundo*."

The man with the hook was startled by the name the younger man gave. He glanced at his brother and saw the same surprise in his eyes. They should have expected this. At least considered the possibility. A long time had passed. A long time. But it had not occurred to them.

Now changes would have to be made. Things would have to be managed in a different manner. It might be even more difficult than they had anticipated, and they'd had no illusions about that from the beginning. They'd have to go gently. Very gently, indeed.

He folded the hook across the horn of his saddle and covered it with his good hand.

"J. Neville, Stanton," he said in self-introduction. "My brother, Blair. We've had a long day. Likely as long a one tomorrow. Seems to go that way in this country. They told us when we left the Trail over east that you might put us up. If it's not too much of an inconvenience."

"Riding grubline?" young Stanton asked.

"I beg your pardon?"

"Looking for work," Jaime Henry cut in shortly. "You're no hands, the way we count 'em here."

"No," J. Neville agreed. "Ex-soldiers, trying to put as much time and distance between us and the stink of the war as we can. We pay our way. For a while longer, anyhow."

"Rebs, eh?" the Stanton foreman grunted.

"Point of view, isn't it?" Neville asked. "Did our time in the Army of the Confederacy. Does it make that much difference out here?"

"Not on the Corona," young Stanton said. "Can't speak for the rest of the Territory. New Mexicans make up their own minds. But no trouble, I'd think, if you don't make any."

"Less'n you're Texans," Jaime Henry warned. "They's still a bounty on them bastards in the back country."

"Virginians," Neville said.

" 'Light down," young Stanton invited. "Hugo'll bait and bed your horses."

He gestured to the black man, who rode over to take the leads as the two strangers swung down.

"My mother's always pleased to have guests at our table," Stanton continued. "Specially from the East. Claims they're her newspaper as to what's going on in the rest of the country."

"We'll try to oblige."

Tito Stanton led the way into the house.

J. Neville found himself in a baronial, stone-flagged hall with a huge fireplace and a broad stair rising to upper rooms. Indian rugs and animal skins were scattered on the floor. One was the largest bear pelt Neville had ever seen. The furniture was deep and massive. It was hand-shaped and pegged and upholstered in thick, studded leather. He realized everything in the room was a product of the ranch.

Tito introduced his guests to his mother, a proud and stately woman with a yet stunningly beautiful face and magnificent figure. She spoke without a trace of accent but Neville saw at once that she was native to this land. Spencer Stanton had found her here, perhaps on the Corona Grant itself.

"I am 'Mana," she said. "To all who know me. From the smallest *niñita* in the village to the *Palacio de los Gobernadores* in Santa Fe. It must be the same with you, *señores*. No, please, I insist. It is my custom."

"No use arguing," young Stanton said with a grin. "In this house her custom is law."

Neville had believed that the pillared plantation hall in which he and Blair had been born and raised was a great and gracious house, but this fortress in the wilderness dimmed its memory. In the same way he remembered some of the grand ladies of his youth, some high queens of fashion in their own right, but none who had captivated him as instantly and utterly as the mistress of the Corona.

'Mana Stanton introduced the newcomers to the two younger children—Quelí, a beautiful girl of sixteen or so who was a reincarnation of her mother, and a big-bodied boy about twelve whom she called Bronco. Blair was immediately attracted to the daughter, but J. Neville's eyes searched for the man they had ridden two-thirds of the way across the country to see.

Tito Stanton seemed to understand. He led the way down the room to a door at the far end. Opening this, he ushered the Nevilles into what in another house would have been a library but was here obviously the ranch office. The man they were seeking arose from a deep reading chair.

Spencer Stanton was a little gray at the temples and he had a slight limp as he moved forward but he was an imposing figure of a man in the prime of life. J. Neville felt the probe of the deep-set eyes and he realized that he and his brother had set themselves a formidable task, indeed. The rancher offered his hand in acknowledgment of his son's introduction.

"Blair—Jay, pleased to have you," he said.

"Not Jay, the name—the word," Neville corrected. "Just J., the initial."

Spencer Stanton's brows rose slightly.

"That's all?" he asked.

Neville nodded.

"Not much of a name."

"It serves."

"Yes," Stanton agreed. "I suppose. A drink?"

He filled three glasses and retrieved his own from beside his chair. His eyes continued to probe the newcomers as he gestured a silent toast with his glass and sipped its contents.

Neville felt the powerful impact of the man. Memory did not suffice. It had been too long ago. Nor did what he and Blair had been told and all they had been able to learn. He felt a grudging wave of respect he neither anticipated nor particularly welcomed.

He glanced at Blair and saw that his brother was in the grip of a similar revelation. At the same instant came a clear, instinctive warning. To attempt to deal in deceit with this man would be utter folly. Disaster before they were fairly begun.

"Actually not Neville, either," he said.

Stanton sipped his whiskey again.

"No?"

"You know who we are."

Stanton's eyes were gimlet-hard.

"Yes," he said quietly. Bitterness harshened his

voice. "A man can rid himself of enemies but he can't destroy his own memories, no matter how hard he tries. He knows his own seed."

"And you know why we're here."

"I think so," Stanton assented. He turned to his son. "Ask Jaime to step in here and close the door, Tito."

Curious, the younger Stanton obeyed and returned with Jaime Henry, shutting the door behind them. There was a moment of silence, the younger men waiting upon the older. Suddenly the glass shattered in Spencer Stanton's hand. He flung the shards into the fireplace, took out a linen kerchief, and absently dabbed at a small cut in his palm.

"These are your half brothers," he told his son. "James and Blair Stanton, whatever they choose to call themselves. They want their share of the Corona."

Chapter 2

Tito Stanton stared incredulously at his father and these two strangers who had come in from the grass. As had been his habit since infancy, he looked at Jaime Henry, too. He saw that Jaime knew these two existed and had known since the beginning. Not where, perhaps, but that they existed. Dark clouds below a distant horizon. He felt a surge of resentment that he had not also known. There had been no secrets kept from him on the ranch or in the family since he could remember.

He had always vaguely understood that Spencer Stanton had once had an earlier life somewhere on the eastern seaboard. It had been long ago. Years before the already forgotten war with Mexico that had cemented New Mexico to the Union. He had accepted this without further curiosity.

It had never occurred to him that there could have been another family. Surely not another woman before his mother. With 'Mana Stanton it was unthinkable.

He saw no kinship between himself and these two. None between them and his father. He could sense no common flesh and blood. Instead, instinct told him these were enemies. Perhaps deadly ones. He felt his hackles rise.

"I don't like the joke," he said. "Or them, now."

"No joke," Stanton said bleakly. "And I don't give a hoot in hell whether you like them or they you. But there's some things to settle before we join the women. We'll air no dirty linen or hard words before them. Not in this house."

"Naturally," the older of the two newcomers agreed. "We're that much gentlemen."

Stanton indicated the hook the other wore in place of his right hand.

"The war?"

"A Yankee Rodman-ball at Shiloh. Bigger than a keg and whistling along so lazily we could see it coming, but we couldn't get out of the way. There were six of us, men and horses. This much of me was all that was left of the lot."

Tito thought that a flicker of approval, even respect, showed briefly in his father's eyes.

"You paid your price," Spencer Stanton said.

"Less than many."

"After the war—how'd you find me?"

Blair Stanton produced a much-folded newspaper clipping and handed it over. Stanton glanced at it and passed it on to Tito. He read into it quickly.

> 'Washington, D. C. Spencer Stanton, sole owner of the Corona Grant, a three-hundred-thousand-acre ranch in northern New Mexico Territory, was commended by Congress in joint session for delivering more than twenty-five thousand head of beef cattle to Grant's commissary during the bitter campaign in the West.
>
> 'Stanton, reputedly the richest and most powerful man in the Territory, was quoted at the end of one of his remarkable drives across the western deserts as offering to strip his range to the last steer if necessary to fill the General's needs . . .'

Tito read no more but passed the clipping to Jaime.

"After Blair ran across that," the man with the hook said, "it was just a matter of getting together and starting west, asking questions along the way."

"Now you're here," Spencer Stanton said. "In my country. I didn't ask for it and sure as hell don't want it. Never did. But you bear my blood. You'll damned well bear my name long as you're in the Territory. To hell with what you do elsewhere. And you'll bear it honorably, by god. No hiding behind a sneaking alias. So men'll know who you are, whatever you aim to do."

"Suits us. It's always been our name. We've been proud enough of it if not of you."

"The first name—I won't have you using Jay, however you spell it or whatever it stands for. Or James or Jim. They belong to Jaime on the Corona. Jim Henry. You said 'Neville' when you rode in. You chose it, now use it. Neville Stanton. Neville and Blair Stanton. Understand?"

"As good as any other—out here," the brother so renamed agreed with a shrug.

"There was another whelp on the way when I left," Spencer Stanton continued. "A bastard sired in your mother's bed when my back was turned."

Neville Stanton glanced at Tito and nodded.

"Another half brother. On our mother's side, as you say. No scandal, really. She married his father shortly after you disappeared. Both the boy and his father were killed fighting off a guerrilla raid across the Virginia border. When he was seventeen."

Stanton was silent a long moment.

"So Belle paid her price, too," he murmured.

Neville nodded, absently clicking the gripping device on his hook with a faint show of impatience.

"She died a few months later, nursing in a Confederate staging hospital. It was nearly a year before either Blair or I knew. The fortunes of war."

"I have no feeling over that," Stanton said harshly.

"None expected—from you."

"You have no feeling for me and expect none in me for you?"

"No. As I said. Neither one of us."

"Then why this fool long ride? Greed—revenge—hate—what?"

"Like it or not, either way you're our father."

"Damn it, I left Belle a valuable property," Stanton

protested. "Everything I had. In spite of what she'd done. Ample means. All yours, now that she's dead—along with the son of a bitch she took into my bed and her child. Surely enough for you both, in spite of the war. We've earned our place here. Jaime, Tito, the rest of my family. You haven't."

"Yet," Neville corrected. "McClellan took the main force of his army straight through the farm in his drive on Richmond. Every head of stock was commandeered. Stanton Hall was sacked and burned to the ground. Dikes were cut to get artillery through and the river ate away the land. There was barely enough salvage to get us here."

"As you said, the fortunes of war."

"No, by god," Neville Stanton said with sudden heat. He waved his hook in his father's face. "This is all I'll accept for that. It's damned well enough. Hell, Blair and I aren't responsible for our mother's mistakes or McClellan's fury. You're our father. We want a patrimony. You owe it. You can afford it. We're going to have it."

Something snapped in Tito at the sight of the flashing steel at the end of the mutilated arm, the seemingly threatening gesture toward the man he respected above all others. No man threatened Spencer Stanton in his son's presence.

Tito took one quick stride forward. He seized the brandishing hook, avoiding its wickedly sharpened point, and jerked his half brother around by it. The tug was so violent that the lacings that bound the appliance to the arm parted and the hook came away in Tito's hand. He flung it from him and hit Neville hard below the ear.

Neville landed on his shoulders and skidded against the wall. Blair Stanton leaped in at Tito. Sidestepping him, Tito hit him twice as he tried to reverse. His knees buckled and he spilled across his brother's legs.

Jaime Henry had not moved.

"Boy, when you learn you learn good," he said in the Missouri drawl that still surfaced when he was pleased.

COMPAÑEROS   21

"You keep your touch. Couldn't a done better myself."

Tito knew if he had not swung on Neville Stanton, Jaime would have done so an instant later. He prodded the men on the floor with the toe of his boot.

"Up, you sons of bitches," he grated. "On your feet and out of the house. Now!"

His father gripped Tito's arm and drew him back, allowing the downed pair room to rise. Tito felt the restraint but saw that Spencer Stanton was not displeased.

Blair Stanton retrieved the hook and handed it to his brother. Neville thrust it back onto the scarred stump of his wrist. He viciously jerked the lacings tight with his good hand and his teeth. When the hook was resecured he glared malevolently at Tito.

"Grab this again and I'll sink it in your gullet!"

"I wouldn't try," Tito said.

His father released Tito's arm.

"That's enough!" Stanton ordered. "Knuckles and hard words are no substitutes for reason. Only when reason fails."

He retrieved and refilled the glasses, taking down another for Jaime and a fresh one for himself. Again he gestured the same silent toast and sipped the whiskey.

"Neville—Blair—you get this," he continued. "Tito's wrong. I'll put no man out of my house who's had a drink with me till he's had the chuck and bed he's been promised. If he minds his manners."

He looked steadily at the Virginians, putting his will upon them.

"You had sense enough to change your mind after you got here and admit who you are, why you're here. That's reason. Within limits I'm a reasonable man. Let's go from there. Sit down. All of you."

Tito and Jaime obeyed. Blair and Neville Stanton sullenly followed suit. Favoring his right leg slightly, Stanton lowered his thickening, powerful frame into his big chair.

"Fact is, you're all my sons, one way or another," he continued. "Jaime, too, if not by blood. It's only right we thresh this out together. With reason. Or try to. Agreed?"

Tito grimly disapproved of his father's tolerance but long training held. He nodded wordless assent. So did Jaime. Blair Stanton looked uncertainly at his brother. Neville shrugged, making no concession.

"Long as the answer comes out right. That's all we give a damn about."

"We'll come to that," Stanton said imperturbably. "But you got some notions you're going to have to get rid of. You think we've made a lot of money here. Great wealth, even."

"You obviously have," Neville said flatly. " 'The richest and most powerful man in the Territory,' that newspaper article says."

"The biggest ranch, anyway," Stanton agreed. "The most land in one chunk. That's what you don't understand. That's riches out here. That's wealth."

"If it makes money," Neville said.

"It does. Some. It'll make a lot more before we're done building. That's why I want to make one thing clear. The Corona will never be apportioned or divided or broken up—even a single five-acre patch split from it—in my lifetime or the lifetimes of my children and their children's children. If that's your idea."

"Worth thinking about," Neville answered with a cutting edge to his voice. "You can't keep on running this ranch the way you do now forever."

"No," Stanton admitted. "Not when my time comes, for whatever reason. But my wife can after me. Jaime can. Tito and even Bronc, when he's grown into his boots. They will, too. Make no mistake about that. It might be fatal."

"Fatal?"

Neville irritably clicked the gripping device on his hook.

"Mother always said you were overbearing. We're not New Mexican peons, knees knocking together in

front of the great man. Blair and I've been through one
hell of a goddamn war. On the battlefields. A lot of
them. We've fought armies, a whole damned nation of
enemies."

"Why not? You're Stantons. On one side, at least."

"That's not the point. You're just one man. So's my
half brother, there. And your foreman. That boy in the
other room. And your wife's a woman. We don't scare."

"You don't know me. Some men bluff. I don't. Neither do I threaten. I just wanted you to know the facts.
That's all."

"The facts are this isn't a Mexican province anymore. It's part of the U.S.A. You may refuse to grant us
our due as your sons but we're citizens of the United
States and entitled to rights under the law."

"On the Corona I'm the law."

"Bullshit," Neville Stanton grunted. "The courts'll
think differently. They're going to have to. There are
thousands of men from both armies drifting this way.
We saw them everywhere. Disillusioned men with pockets full of worthless scrip issued them for mustering-out
pay. Every man-jack looking for someplace to light and
make a new beginning."

"There's room."

"You're damned right. Right here. You're sitting on
enough land to resettle them all. And no proof of ownership but mere possession and a title issued by the for-
eign government of a former national enemy. One man
against thousands. Hard case to win. Especially when
the one's rich and the rest penniless."

"It can be done. When the time comes."

"The hell it can!" Neville Stanton exploded. "You're
supposed to be an educated man. History tells you how
it'll come out. How it's got to. How it always has. The
have-nots'll get. You can't risk that."

"Boy, you do try a man," Spencer Stanton said. Only
Tito and Jaime knew how close he was to the limit of
his patience. "I've been trying to explain to you. We

don't read history in this country. We're too damned
busy making it. And you keep jumping the gun a mile
on me. I aim to grant you your due, as you call it."

Jaime Henry's jaw slackened with astonishment and
Tito Stanton stared at his father in disbelief. Well as
they knew Spencer Stanton, they had not expected this.
He was a fair man by most standards but he was hard-
chilled steel when it came to anything affecting the Corona and those upon it.

Blair Stanton leaned forward, excited relief in his
eyes. However, his brother looked at Spencer Stanton in
hard, shrewd speculation. Tito knew he was the more
dangerous of the two.

"Equal shares?" Neville asked warily.

"Wouldn't have it any other way," Stanton agreed
amiably. "Same as the rest of us. Same I'd grant any
other pair of able-bodied men who came to me honestly
wanting to make their own way and build their own
lives. Same chance I had when I came out here. Same
as Jaime and Tito and Bronc. Same as any hand on the
ranch, according to his worth and ambition."

"Words!" Neville scoffed.

"With meaning. I've tried to tell you. We don't have
wealth here the way you mean. Money, gold, whatever.
There isn't a hundred dollars hard cash within a
hundred miles of this house. What we do have is a god-
awful lot of hard work staring us in the face if we're
going to get done what has to be done. We'll sure as hell
share that, even-Steven, daylight to dark. And no com-
plaints."

Relief flooded Tito. Jaime winked at him. The Missourian's eyes were dancing with amusement. In the
truculent tension of this unexpected and unwanted confrontation, they had forgotten that Spencer Stanton
could also be a very devious and misleading man.

Neville Stanton surged angrily to his feet.

"Goddamn it, I told you we're not peons!" he protested. "Even your foreman had sense enough to know
we're no damned hired hands, either. We didn't come

out here looking for jobs or a crock of two-bit advice."

"Been smarter," Stanton said calmly. "Advice is free. You're both still wet enough behind the ears to use a little. Out here, anyway. And for your information, a man on a working cattle ranch doesn't have to look very far for jobs. If he just stands still for thirty seconds, jobs'll find him. More'n he can handle."

He finished his drink and stood up.

"That's the way it is. You takes it or you leaves it."

Neville slammed his glass down on the table beside which he was standing.

"You can go to hell!"

"Probably will," Stanton agreed with a smile. "In due time. I've been invited often enough. But right now we're going in to supper. 'Mana's table is one thing on the Corona that won't wait for godalmighty himself."

He paused at the door before opening it.

"Eat hearty," he added. "If you're as stony as you claim it may be a while before you do again. In spite of what you may have heard about hospitality out here, damned few doors are open anymore to strangers with empty pockets. On general principles. Something the *paisanos* have had to learn since the *yanquis* came."

Chapter 3

Neville Stanton was not impressed with Santa Fe. It seemed incredible that this flat-roofed mud town, sleeping in the dust of time, could be the fountainhead of the fabled Santa Fe trade. There was less activity in the drowsy plaza here at high noon of a business day than before a Virginia backwoods crossroads store at Sunday vespers.

Keeping his hook discreetly hidden in his jacket pocket as he habitually did in public places, he pulled up as he had been directed before the Palace of the Governors on the north side of the unplanted dirt square. The building impressed him no more than the rest of the town. Although it had an extensive front of several hundred feet, shaded by a wide veranda, it was the same single-story, flat-roofed adobe construction as most of the other buildings in the territorial capital.

However, there was treasure within. He was convinced of that. Or, rather, the means to treasure, if he could lay his hands on it. Powerful as the Corona and its master were, even more powerful forces could be brought to bear upon them. In the end, even as arrogant and stubborn a man as Spencer Stanton could be forced to realize it would be cheaper to accept his sons than deny them.

Blair pulled up beside him the one packhorse they had brought into town with them on lead. Neville spoke to him.

"Drop my horse at that livery we passed over on the next street. Have them grain it up against a hard ride in case I have to run for it. I'll pick it up shortly after dark."

"You sure this is going to work?" Blair asked uneasily.

"I wish to hell you were as confident in the saddle as you are in some doxie's bed," Neville growled. "Where's the tiger of Company C? I didn't hear you come up with something better and we've got to start someplace, don't we? In a hurry."

"I don't know. In a country that's strange to us, J. . . ."

"Neville. Remember? If the old man's setting the rules we'll damned well play by them. Our way. Strange country around Antietam, too, but we rode in and we rode out. Find a store and lay in what we'll need for a few weeks. Shoot the works. Whatever's left in the kitty."

"We do and we may be on our ass tomorrow."

"Tomorrow'll take care of itself. Today's all we've got to worry about. Get going."

Neville swung down and handed over his reins. Blair indicated a storefront across the plaza, next to the Corona Trust and Guaranty Company. The sign above it read: WETZEL Y CIA.

"No," Neville said. "Someplace else. If that wagon master told us right out on the pass yesterday, I just may be talking to Mr. Wetzel and Company a little later. We don't want to give him all our trade. Get what we need and out of town as soon as you can. Hole up where we left the packs and the other horse. I should be there by midnight. Daylight at the latest."

"Be careful."

"I'd rather be rich."

Blair kicked up his horse and rode across the plaza, leading the other two animals. No curious eye followed him. Neville sauntered across the walk under the veranda of the Palace of the Governors and casually entered the building.

The very courteous old custodian of the records and the pretty, big-breasted girl who was his assistant found the documents in the archives with little difficulty. They brought out the huge old vellum volumes and opened them before Neville on a chest-high, slant-topped pine table.

They did not seem curious at his interest and left him alone to peruse the records at his leisure. Apparently it was no uncommon thing these days for Yankee strangers to want to search through the musty pages bearing the legal history of ownership and transaction in Spanish and Mexican times.

Spencer Stanton's confidence in the security of his title to the Corona Grant seemed justified by the record. Not altogether to his surprise, Neville discovered his father had received it by deed of spouse from a Mexican woman who in turn had it by inheritance in a direct line from the original grantee who had received it from a king of Spain nearly two hundred years before.

Plainly the Mexican woman was the one now known as 'Mana Stanton. Neville realized that her interest and those of her children by Stanton would supersede in the eyes of any fair-minded court any claim he and Blair could put forward through their father. Even the far more liberal law of the American Republic would be bound to treat a line of succession and inheritance as ancient and continuous as this with the respect to which it was doubtless due.

Although there was no indication that a territorial court had yet reviewed this title, Stanton's position was further solidified by the fact it had been confirmed by a Manuel Armijo, provincial governor under Mexico, soon after his marriage to the Mexican woman who was now his wife. On the face of it, to attempt to exert any pressure on Spencer Stanton from this direction would have little hope of effectiveness.

There was a further complication. Some twenty miles to the south of the main body of the Corona Grant was another large deeded tract along the base of the mountains. This Rancho Mora was also in Spencer Stanton's name but only as trustee for his son Roberto, who had received it—apparently in infancy—by deed of gift upon the death of a Felipe Peralta, the former owner, identified as Roberto Stanton's godfather. The unbroken line of succession on this property was equally as long and Stanton's trusteeship would end at Tito's majority. Neville thought this must be at any time now.

His half brother's title to the lower ranch would then be fully as sound as was his father's and mother's to the upper tract of the Corona. Again there was no valid bloodline by which it could be assailed.

Both might be challenged in time as the Territory moved toward statehood, but only by the most powerful interests. The railroads, perhaps, when they came. Or the government, itself, righteously trying to strike down individuals who held too much of this new country. But certainly not Blair and Neville Stanton, however cleverly they planned.

Bitterly disappointed, angry that he could find no chink into which he could drive a wedge to accomplish what he wanted, Neville was about to close the musty old folios when something about a meticulously hand-drawn plat that located the two grants which were now the Stanton ranch caught his attention. This was the roughly twenty-mile gap between the boundaries of the two. It was blank, unmarked by salient features, identified only as *malpaís*.

Latin from schooling interrupted by the war lifted meaning from the Spanish word. *Mal-país*—bad land. Suddenly it all dropped into place. Here, too, was something that would hold up in a court of law, in public opinion, and in the judgment of all fair-minded men. Here was something easier, surer, and far less dangerous than the campaign he and Blair had planned.

Taking up a pen from the desk and a sheet of paper that had been left with him for notes, Neville Stanton began to carefully trace off the plat, accurately reproducing scale and notations.

Quitting the Corona to rejoin the Santa Fe Trail, their father had given Blair and himself a landmark to the southeast to ride toward to save themselves considerable time and distance on their way to the capital. Stanton had called it Fire Mountain. It was a symmetrical cinder cone, standing completely apart and towering high above the flat horizon of grass.

Later, when they had rounded it to the east as they had been instructed and picked up the rutted breadth of the Trail to Sante Fe, they had seen a vast, dismal area of tumbled lava that had spewed from the cone in some ancient time. It extended miles to the south and apparently almost to the foot of the mountains to the west. To all appearances, it was impassable or nearly so.

By the plat, the southeastern boundary marker of the original Corona Grant was on the summit of Fire Mountain. It became obvious why the vacant strip of emptiness lay between the grant and Tito Stanton's inherited Rancho Mora. The first grantees, in making their petition to the Spanish king, had seen no reason to include such worthless land within the boundaries of either tract. Neither had anyone else. As a result, the *malpaís* area had remained ungranted and unclaimed. It doubtless was so still.

Struggling with unfamiliar measurements as reflected on the plat, Neville at length concluded that the portion of the area he thought would be adequate for his purposes covered about ten thousand Spanish *hectáreas*. Closing the old books, he found the big-breasted girl in the anteroom and asked her for a conversion to English acres.

It seemed to be a familiar request to her. Beckoning him close so he could see the computation over her shoulder, she worked figures on a pad. Neville was distracted because he could see somewhat more from this position. She straightened after a moment and smiled.

He realized she was aware of the direction of his gaze and not at all displeased.

"There you are, *señor*," she said. "It comes to about twenty-five thousand acres. Slightly less."

"Thank you."

"*De nada.*"

He turned toward the door, thinking that there had been a flicker of disappointment in her eyes as he left. He went out into the sun of the plaza, carefully folding the plat to fit within his shirt. Twenty-five thousand acres—that could be managed, he believed. If worst came to worst it could be done with somewhat less, although perhaps not as effectively.

It might be impossible for Blair and himself to force Spencer Stanton to some sort of recognition of their claim against him by legal attack upon the family titles to his ranch. But here was means to pose a more compelling threat. If legal control and possession of those unwanted badlands could be secured, the Stanton ranch could be cut in two and all communication between Mora and the Corona proper brought to a halt.

Neville believed he knew how that could be done, quietly and without forewarning. It would take a little money. Perhaps quite a bit for this country if his father had been right about the shortage of cash here. Still, he thought enough could be had. But not in broad daylight. He would have to kill time until shadows lengthened and evening came on.

He thought of the girl in the archives office and the full brown breasts he had looked down upon while she made her calculations. He thought of her smile and the shadow of disappointment in her eyes. It would be a pleasant way to pass a time of waiting. It would be a simple matter of faking interest in further information, perhaps of going back into some private corner of the musty old stacks with her in search of it. But that was for Blair.

Blair was expert at this. His success was phenomenal, his appetite never sated. It was a game with him, more challenging and exciting than the highest stakes at cards. And he played it as ruthlessly as any gambler. Willingness in his victim was not necessary, only acquiescence. It had always been this way with Blair. The war had only hardened him and made him more aggressive. It was an unfair deception. None of this showed in the handsome face, splendid body, and usually courtly manner.

In a way Neville Stanton envied his brother. On occasion women stirred him just as powerfully. But he was handicapped. Sooner or later his missing hand had to be revealed and it was invariably repellent. The one thing he could not do with his hook was deliver a caress, however much he might desire to.

He was as hard a man as Blair. Even harder in many ways. More given to anger, passion, and lust as well, he supposed. But it was not in his nature to dominate the helpless for whatever purpose.

He turned his back on the Palace of the Governors and crossed the plaza to the southeastern corner. A large, low inn called La Fonda reached back into lesser buildings there and the corner itself was occupied by a tavern with windows, now shuttered against the sun, opening in French style onto the promenade of the square.

Entering the dark, cool interior, he took a table near the shuttered, glassless windows. Knowing he might otherwise be occupied at the supper hour, he ordered a drink and a full meal. It seemed a good way to spend the last gold coin in his pocket. That was a shortage he would shortly remedy. And it would pass the time.

Neville lingered over his drink, had another, and ate in New Mexican style, without haste. Afterward he unhurriedly finished the really quite good bottle of table wine with which he had been provided. When he paid his chit and left the table the sun was down and the floor-length shutters on that side of the room had been opened to the twilight settling over the plaza. He stepped through one of these into the square.

With the passing of the sun Santa Fe had roused to life. The perimeter of the plaza was filling with strollers on the walks before the fronting buildings. Although the older people walked in pairs and mingled in groups to stop and chat, Neville saw with amusement that the young and unattached remained separated by sex. The boys and young men circulated in one direction, the girls and younger women in the other.

There was no exchange between them except when they met and passed the particular objects of their interest. There were quick smiles and an occasional giggle then. Neville wondered how courtship was contrived under such an arrangement. It would hardly be to Blair's satisfaction, but he was grateful himself for the casual cover it afforded him and he fell in with the parade of unattached males.

Part of the way around he encountered the girl from the archives walking with another. She spotted him and smiled brightly as she passed. Neville responded but continued on as did the others.

He was glad his brother was not with him. This was no time for dalliance. He had no interest beyond a sufficient study of the lay of the land before he made his move.

On the next circuit of the plaza the girl had separated from her companion. When she saw him approaching a second time she stepped into an unlighted doorway and looked out invitingly from the shadows there. Neville touched his hat to her in passing but did not pause. In the mirror of a storefront glass he saw her flounce from the doorway and rejoin the other girl, shoulders swinging in disdainful pique.

The second time he passed the Wetzel and Company store, a final customer was emerging with a purchase and a small, ageless man with a stiff shock of white hair was briskly beginning to trim down lamps within. He judged this to be the proprietor and that he was pre-

paring to close for the night. If so, he knew he would
have to watch his timing closely from here on.

He lifted his stride and turned out of the plaza at the
next corner into a narrow passage. This led to the next
street and the livery to which he had directed Blair. His
horse was ready. He had a moment of misgiving over
his carelessness in spending his last sou in the La Fonda
tavern, but he discovered Blair had thought to pay the
livery fee in advance.

He felt a flash of gratitude. In most things they
worked well together, each automatically covering for
the other. Even in small things such as this.

Mounting, Neville rode back into the plaza, working
his horse through the promenaders and back up past the
Wetzel store and the Corona Trust and Guaranty Company to a use-polished tie-rack just beyond. He checked
his girth, left his horse there, and rejoined the strollers.
Fortunately he did not encounter the girl from the archives again.

The last light in the Wetzel store went out. The little
man with the shock of white hair emerged with a big
brass ring of keys. As he was locking the store a passerby spoke to him, calling him by name, and Neville
grinned with satisfaction. This was, as he hoped, the
man he wanted—Saul Wetzel, Spencer Stanton's partner in several enterprises.

Wetzel went briskly next door to the Corona Trust
and Guaranty Company, which was still open, and disappeared within. Neville eased from the parade of
strollers and leaned casually against the front of the
building as though weary of promenading. From this
position, with a slight turn of the head, he had a view of
the interior of the bank.

Wetzel seemed to have a standard routine. He shot
an inside bolt on the street door, pulled down the two
hanging lobby lamps, and snuffed them in sign of closing. He took the day's work sheets and their cashboxes
from the two clerks behind the grille and went back to a
desk beside the big safe at the rear.

Sitting down there, he began counting the contents of the cashboxes and reconciling them with the work sheets. Presently he came forward with the clerks when they were ready and let them out the front door, shooting the bolt behind them again. Snuffing the rest of the lamps but the one over the desk at the rear, he returned to it and resumed his accounting.

Neville waited patiently, pleased that it was growing darker in the plaza. In a few minutes Wetzel lifted down a big ledger and made the day's entries in it. He put the cashboxes, work sheets, and ledger into the big safe, slammed it shut, and spun the dial. With a careful look about to see that all else was in order, he snuffed the last lamp and moved to the street door.

Neville remained motionless until Wetzel emerged and turned with his ring of keys to lock the door for the night. Sliding the gun holstered at his left thigh into the clear, Neville pushed away from the wall against which he had been leaning. He forced himself to saunter casually but he held his breath until he was close enough to Wetzel's back for their bodies to screen the gun between them from passing view. He thrust the muzzle firmly against Wetzel's spine before he could turn the tumblers of the lock with his keys.

"Don't turn," Neville ordered softly. "Don't move. Don't make a sound or I'll blow you in two. Back inside. Quietly."

Chapter 4

Wetzel was a prudent man. He did exactly as he was told, stepping back into the darkened bank. Pressing close behind him, Neville shouldered the door closed and shot the interior bolt with his hook. He prodded Wetzel on.

"The safe," he said. "Keep looking straight ahead."

Again Wetzel obeyed, passing through the gate in the railing into the rear area. He stopped before the safe and stood rigid and motionless. Again Neville prodded with the gun.

"Open it. No light. You can do it by ear."

Wetzel bent close to the dial of the combination. He turned it carefully. Neville could hear the soft clicking of the tumblers. The sound ceased. Wetzel took the bar handle and depressed it firmly. Internal bolts slid back and the door swung open.

"Six thousand dollars," Neville said, naming the sum he had roughly worked out over his meal at the tavern. "Gold."

Wetzel hesitated and spoke for the first time.

"Don't be a bigger fool than you've already been. One yell and the whole plaza'll be in here. The money in this safe belongs to a lot of them."

"Not all of it. What I want belongs to you and your partner, Spencer Stanton. Count it out. A yell or one false move and you're dead. Don't make a mistake."

Wetzel shrugged and reluctantly knelt before the safe. Neville squatted close behind him to avoid revealing himself and kept the pressure of the gun steady against the man's back. Wetzel lifted out a couple of five-hundred-dollar rolls of wrapped double eagles.

"Where?" he asked, very careful not to turn his head.

"The floor'll do," Neville told him. "Don't take all night about it."

The heavy rolls thumped softly as they were put down. Wetzel lifted out others, adding them to the stack. Directly he stopped.

"A dozen rolls," he said. "Six thousand."

Neville realized there was several times that sum in the safe. He also realized the man before him knew he did. He increased the pressure of the gun.

"On your feet," he ordered.

Wetzel rose carefully, ramrod stiff.

"Got a kerchief?" Neville asked.

For answer Wetzel cautiously reached back and pulled a bandanna from his hip pocket.

"Tie it over your eyes. Tight."

Wetzel obeyed, knotting the cloth at the back of his head.

"You're crazy," he said. "You haven't a chance of getting out of town."

"Well, I sure as hell can't stay here. Shut the safe and lock it."

The iron door swung closed and the combination dial spun.

"Hell of a bank robber you are," the blindfolded man said. "Six thousand. No more and no less. Why? If it's any of my business."

"It is," Neville told him. "Call it a loan. You might get it back in the long run. Maybe even at a reasonable profit, if you don't make too much of an uproar over getting it back in a hurry. But just to make sure I'm going to tie you up. Hands behind you, now."

Neville withdrew the gun and silently holstered it. Wetzel obediently crossed his hands at the small of his back. Neville reached around him and snaked off his belt. Taking care that his hook avoided the man's flesh, he knotted the belt tightly about the crossed wrists.

Pulling down the still warm lamp above the desk, he jerked the weighted cord from which it hung loose from its ceiling pulley and deftly caught the counterbalance as it fell. He ordered Wetzel to lie on his belly on the floor and drew the man's ankles up, lashing them securely to the crossed wrists with the cord.

"You wait a good half hour before you yell for help," he warned.

"Like hell I will," Wetzel growled. "Just wait till you hit that door."

"It's either that or a bash over the head to put you to sleep for a spell. Take it or leave it."

"Some choice!" the man on the floor snorted. "For six thousand dollars, yet! All right. Half an hour. For what it's worth, I'm a man of my word when I give it."

"An honest banker, by god," Neville said. "A pleasure to do business with you."

Kneeling before the safe, he opened his shirt and transferred the coin-rolls on the floor to the long-flattened pockets of the moneybelt he yet wore. He rose, refastened his shirt, and moved swiftly to the door. Awaiting a suitable interval between two of the now thinning groups of promenaders on the walk, he shot the bolt on the door back and let himself out into the plaza.

He leaned against the wall beside the door for a few moments, as though idling until he was certain his emergence from the Corona Trust and Guaranty Company had not been noted. Behind him Saul Wetzel remained silent, making no attempt to sound an alarm.

Neville was grateful. Granted that Wetzel must regard him as a rank amateur or a decidedly unusual professional when it came to bank-robbing, the trader-banker was an unusual man himself under the circumstances. Apparently he was indeed a man of his word.

So much the better. Neville had not wanted to do violence if it could be avoided. Not that he had any particular distaste for harsh physical measures when

necessary. The war had pretty well drained him of such
niceties. But it was best for his plan and its chances of
ultimate success that he and Blair make no unnecessary
enemies.

Pushing away from the wall, he moved unhurriedly to
his horse, mounted, and rode from the plaza at a casual,
ambling walk that drew no attention.

Their camp was in a secluded draw back from the
freight road at the mouth of Glorieta Pass, about fifteen
miles out of Santa Fe. There was a rill of sweet water
sufficient for their needs and their stock. There was adequate timber for cover and fuel.

Not far distant was a place called Johnson's Ranch,
actually no ranch at all but the first stage and freight
station east of Santa Fe on the Trail. From this spot
they could watch westward traffic along the Trail without being conspicuous themselves. This would now become more important than Neville had realized when he
had selected the campsite on their way into the territorial capital. They would have business to do with selected travellers drifting west along this wilderness high-
way.

Neville made out the glow of the fire from a quarter
of a mile away but he saw Blair had it carefully
screened from direct view. This pleased him. Blair
could be careless, a little too hasty on occasion, particularly when he was on his own. Still, old campaign hab-
its, hard-learned, were not easily forgotten.

He had further proof of this while he was still a
hundred yards or so out into the night. The latch of a
weapon being warningly pulled to full cock sounded almost at his stirrup.

"Sing out!" came the sibilant warning.

"Neville, Blair."

Blair stepped from the black shadow of a clump of
brush, letting down the hammer of his gun.

"You could have whistled 'Dixie' or something," he
complained.

"Expecting enemies?"

"No. Just wasn't anxious for any unexpected company. How'd it go?"

"Not the way we hoped, but better, I think. His titles are good but he overlooked something that'll put him right in our hands if we can fit it together."

"The hell with him. It's some of that good living I want to get my hands on."

"It'll come. Wait'll we get into the light. I've got a little surprise to show you."

"Yeah, well I guess I do, too," Blair said hesitantly. "You got here a little sooner than I expected. You said midnight or later."

"Luck ran better than I expected."

"About time."

Blair turned back to the fire. Neville reined after him. As he rode around screening brush into the circle of light he saw the reason for his brother's hesitancy. A woman was beside the fire. The business between them was finished. She was clothed and stepping back into her *huaraches*. She shot Neville a sullen, defiant look as he swung down angrily.

"You damned fool," he said to Blair, "we've got a hard enough row to hoe without this! These people set store by their women."

"Not this one. She works the kitchen at Johnson's and beds the trade on the side. I met her down on the Trail on the way back and we made us a deal for after work. Nobody knows she's up here and she's going to be too busy to talk when she gets back. A bunch of Johnny Blue drifters rode into the station after dark."

"How many?"

"Maybe a dozen, the ruckus they were making."

"Lay up any whiskey in town?"

"Some," Blair agreed. "The works, you said."

"Any money left?"

"A little."

Neville indicated the woman.

"Pay her."

Blair counted out the few coins remaining in his pocket. The woman watched avariciously.

"It's too damned much," Blair protested. "I can tell you that."

"Pay her," Neville repeated.

Blair dropped the coins into the woman's palm. Her fingers closed eagerly over them. She eyed Neville uncertainly.

"Think you can pick out the leader of those bluecoats that came into the station tonight—the big honcho or whatever you call it?"

She nodded.

"All right. Get him to follow you. I don't give a damn how. But not to the stable or the hayrick or wherever. Up here, understand? Tell him there's free drinks to be had or a young girl with a specialty—anything. But bring him back here, alone."

The woman opened her hand and looked at the coins in it.

"For this?" she asked.

"For that."

"For this, *señor,* I will bring them all, one at a time, and be the young girl, too, if that is wanted."

"It is not wanted. Just the one. The leader. Make sure of that. And don't be all night about it."

"Si, señor. Muy pronto."

The woman whispered swiftly off on her *huaraches* and vanished into the night.

Blair stared incredulously and a little resentfully at Neville.

"Now, for chrissakes, what in the hell was that?" he growled.

"That, my long-peckered partner, is the first step in buying us twenty-five thousand acres of open land right in the middle of Spencer Stanton's rancho."

"Buy!" Blair snorted. "With what?"

"This—"

Neville opened his shirt, snaked out his laden moneybelt, and tossed it down on the blanket at his brother's feet.

"Six thousand dollars gold from the bank we heard the old man owns with a trader named Saul Wetzel in Santa Fe."

"They let you have it?"

"With a little persuasion."

"Now, that's style. I'd have liked it. Damn it, why cut me out?"

"Wouldn't have if I'd known it was coming up. But it went smooth as silk. No way for Wetzel to know who the hell braced him. I never showed my face—or my hook. And he was a smart old bastard. Real cooperative."

Blair dropped to his knees beside the belt, tumbled a coin-roll from one of the pockets, and spilled the minted gold from its wrapper, fingering it sensuously.

"Beautiful," he said. "Been a long time. But six thousand—what good's that on the Corona, the way they're set up? Couldn't buy the doormat with it."

"We won't be buying from them. And when we start trading for land it won't be with gold. Something more valuable, these days, for those who know how to use it. Break out a bottle and be patient. You'll see. I've figured it all out."

The woman from the kitchen at Johnson's Station returned in less than an hour. She had a man with her. A big, hard-eyed man, badly scarred with pox. He was dressed in some shabby remnants of Union Army uniform, much in want of laundering. His arm was about the woman, feeling for a breast as they moved. She was simpering up at him, leading him on so effectively that he was unaware of the two men hunkering with tin cups beside the fire until he was well into the light and it was too late to retreat.

He froze then, angrily thrusting the woman so violently from him that she stumbled to her knees. She remained there, crouching fearfully as his hand went to his gun. Neville Stanton lifted his own ready weapon from his lap.

"I wouldn't," he said quietly. "Come on over peaceably and you can leave the same way directly, with a little whiskey in your belly and profit in your pocket."

The muzzle of the pistol indicated the bottle before Blair and himself and the moneybelt and opened roll of double-eagles still on the blanket.

The man came up warily, glaring at the cowering woman as he passed.

"Damn bitch," he growled. "This sure ain't what she promised. What the hell you want with me?"

"Your name, for starters," Neville told him, signalling Blair toward the bottle and dismissing the woman with his eyes. She understood and scuttled hastily back into the night.

Blair spilled whiskey into another cup and offered it up. The man took it.

"Ted Crane," he said. "Bull sergeant till I mustered out."

"Sit down, Crane. Be sociable."

The man lowered himself, showing cupidity in spite of himself as he eyed the loose gold on the blanket.

"They issue your outfit scrip when they mustered you out?" Neville asked.

"What else? Sure as hell no bonus money or even half the back pay we'd ought to had coming. Damn shinplasters to buy a hundred and sixty acres of bottoms at two-forty an acre or three-twenty on the dry benches at a buck two-bits for every man-jack. That's the grateful, goddamned government for you!"

"Got any of yours left?"

"Sure," Crane agreed, "but damn if I know why I keep it. Good bottoms were long before the war and no man in his right mind'd want a little dab of rock hill or brush and rattlesnakes."

"Mind if I take a look at it?"

"It sure ain't no curiosity, friend," Crane answered. "Every man on the Trail's got a pocketful these days, for what good it does him."

The ex-sergeant reached inside his filthy shirt and pulled out a thin, worn oilskin packet. He fumbled this open and withdrew a crumpled sheaf of government paper, irregularly folded. Neville glanced at it for identification only, realizing Crane's oilskin contained precious little else. The man was hard down on his uppers. He supposed his companions were, too.

"What's it worth?" Neville asked.

"I told you. Nothing. Lord knows we've all tried to trade it off for something. Beans and bacon. Anything. A roll in the hay, even. Let alone some kind of a stake to get to California or Oregon or some place where a man'd have half a chance to get started again. So here I'm stuck in this godforsaken place with damned little budge left to my butt."

"I'll give you twenty cents on the dollar—twenty-four cents an acre for every three-hundred-and-twenty-acre certificate."

"Cash money?"

Neville indicated the gold on the blanket.

"There's the color of it."

"Man, I can get you all you want for half that!"

"That's the idea. I want all the scrip I can get up to twenty-five thousand acres. Twenty-four cents to you. The money's all right there. What you pay for it is up to you, but you shouldn't have to walk the rest of the way to California if you can find me enough."

Crane knocked off the last of the whiskey in his cup and surged eagerly to his feet.

"Mister," he said, "you stay right here. You stay right here!"

He turned and slogged off into the night at a half-run.

Blair refilled Neville's cup and his own.

"Brother," he said admiringly, "not to unduly assault

the memory of our late mother, you are a thoroughgo-
ing son of a bitch!"

"That makes two of us," Neville agreed, "as Spencer
Stanton and our inhospitable half-relations are shortly
going to discover."

Chapter 5

Jaime Henry boasted a perverse theory about the relative intelligence of range beef stock and the wiry, fast-footed horses with which it was customarily worked. He held that the range steer had it over the horse seven ways from Sunday, a blasphemy that horrified the *vaqueros*. Jaime had a pat answer for them. If the horse was so damned smart he'd be out there on the grass stoking his belly all day long and cowboys would be forking cattle or hiking on their own hoofs.

Tito privately felt the Corona *segundo* had a point. He had seen steers—sometimes a whole damned bunch of them in deliberate concert—pull an ingenious piece of utter cussedness no self-respecting cow pony could have thought up in a million years. And he'd seen even the best horses do some almighty dumb things, usually when least expected and with no excuse whatever.

It was an arguable question and was frequently chewed over with some heat when a chuck-fire was lit and there wasn't much else to do or talk about. Next to women it was the favorite subject on such occasions. But there was universal agreement that there was one thing a beef critter was hands down out in front a mile about in any cowman's book. That was laziness.

Unless spooked or occasionally stampeding just for the hell of it, range cattle would eat the best graze in the world right down to the sod before they'd move a hundred yards on their own. The endless and most thankless job on the ranch was to keep them moving to protect the grass. It was an infuriating necessity when so much untouched forage was often but yards away. So

they grudgingly took their turns as chance dictated, riding their brass-bound butts sore.

Tito had been hazing small bunches all day, a few
rods here and half a mile there. His arm was sore from
smacking their rumps with a doubled length of *reata* to
get their heads up and make them foot along at a reasonable rate. It was dog work and did little for his dis-
position.

He pulled up on the low, barely discernible rise on
the eastward grass that separated the drainages of
Conejo Creek and the Cimarroncito and looked back at
the area he had been working. He thought the bunches
satisfactorily redistributed and the job well enough done
for now. As he kicked his horse up again he saw, off
toward the mountains, two horses tied to bank-brush
beside the Cimarroncito, a few miles south of headquarters.

It meant a detour but at this distance he could not
tell if they were Corona stock and he didn't think any of
the hands had been assigned day-chores in that area.
Everyone seemed to have dismissed them from mind
but Tito could not forget the brief presence of his two
half brothers and their unrepentant hostility on departure over the choice their father had offered them. He
was in no mood for other strangers on the ranch.

He turned his weary horse into a shallow draw that
would take him by the easiest and quickest route to the
banks of the Cimarroncito. In a quarter of a mile the
gentle swells between which the draw ran had risen to
obscure his destination. He rode on, lost in his own
thoughts and letting his horse set its own pace.

There was a willow thicket at the mouth of the draw
where it reached the Cimarroncito. Tito's pony threaded
it, deftly avoiding the slender, whiplike branches that
could put a welt on a man through his shirt if they
caught him right. As a result, his approach was silent, if
not intentionally so. He pulled up at the edge of the
willows as the two saddled horses he had seen from
higher ground came into view.

His concern had been needless. Both wore the crown-shaped brand of the Corona. The Cimarroncito, barely a dozen yards wide and shin-deep in most places, ran in a shallow cutbank here, making a lazy turn at an almost lawnlike patch of short, soft summer grass below the brush where the horses were tied.

In the middle of this inviting patch of natural turf were two heaps of clothing—unmistakably women's clothing. And there was laughing and giggling and splashing under the cutbank where there was deeper water on the inside of the turn.

Tito had been about to ride on into the open. Now he checked his horse again and sat motionless, reasonably well hidden in the fringe of the willows. It was a wise precaution.

In only moments the two naked bathers came splashing up out of the stream. He saw with no particular surprise that they were his sister Quelí and Greta, Jaime and Helga Henry's daughter. Except at roundup time, when Jaime could not afford the extra riding entailed, the Henrys lived in the comfortable old Spanish adobe near the mouth of Cimarron Canyon where 'Mana Ruíz had been born. It had been her home until the coming of Spencer Stanton.

The girls were usually together at one house or the other and frequently rode out onto the grass on adventures of their own. Greta Henry was the oldest by about two years. She had her mother's heavy golden braids as Quelí had 'Mana's magnificent hip-length fall of gleaming jet-black hair. In this the contrast between them was startling. In all else they were so close as to have been sisters.

Still laughing in pure exuberance, they flung themselves down on the grass to let the dry air and low sun dry their glistening bodies before they dressed.

Tito was a Stanton. He had no particular compunction about watching while not making his presence known. There were two reasons for this.

As far as Quelí was concerned, she was his sister.

They had grown up together in a household where privacy was rigidly respected insofar as possible but the human as well as the animal world about them was accepted honestly and naturally as it was, day to day, without cloying mysteries and false modesties.

He did not remember when, but it had been a long time since he had seen Quelí as she now was. As a young child, probably, on a bath night or some such necessary and common occasion. His only reaction now was a startled realization that she had already become so much a woman. That was important here in the high country. It was just as important as a boy becoming a man—as men were measured here.

Her body was beautiful in its promise. A promise already realized enough for any man. Her breasts were rounded and swelling, nipples erectile in the warm sun. Her belly was flat, her thighs and hips gracefully curved, her pubic hair as luxuriant as that upon her head. Still a child in laughter but a woman in all else. He felt a new surge of pride in her. She, too, was a Stanton and her mother's daughter.

Greta Henry was something else. She had also been a sister when they were younger. But that had passed with the years and both of them were aware of it. Tito knew he had been watching her with rising interest as time went on. He didn't know if she was aware of that.

What she couldn't know was that when he sometimes succeeded in closing his mind to other things he could see her there. Not as she now was here on the grass. Not that this wasn't what he often mightily wanted; he was just unable to summon the vision. Even if he had, it would not have been like this.

She was a larger girl than Quelí in all ways, with a fuller body. Her heavy breasts thrust firmly, proudly toward the sky. Her seeking nipples stood higher, a delicate pink. From the fairness of her skin, he supposed. Her belly was gently rounded over firm muscles. Her hips swelled excitingly from her small waist and her legs were long and straight.

It had long been accepted on the Corona, perhaps from the earliest days of their childhood, that Spencer and 'Mana Stanton's son and Jaime and Helga Henry's daughter would one day be man and wife. The procreation of the dynasty. For a long time Tito had known he loved Greta—as he loved Quelí. He had supposed that would be enough when the time came. He knew now that it would not.

With a heightening of every sense in his being he knew that he had to have this. All that lay there on the grass with his sister. He knew it was lust, for it shook him to his roots. But the Stantons were a lusty clan. This was the way they fell in love.

In a few minutes Quelí and Greta rose and dressed. They mounted their horses and rode out, passing quite near the willows in which Tito sat on his motionless horse. As they did so he thought with a sudden stab of alarm that Greta looked straight at him. However, there was no change in her expression and he eased as they continued on.

When the sound of their horses faded he rode out onto the patch of turf where they had dried themselves. As soon as he showed himself another horseman rode out of the brush a little upstream from where the girls had tied their mounts. The rider came purposefully straight toward him. With a heavy sinking of spirit he saw that it was Jaime Henry. He wanted no confrontation but it looked like he had no choice.

Jaime drew alongside. Both pulled up. The Missourian's eyes were unreadable.

"Looking for something?" he asked.

Tito nodded, unwilling to trust his voice after the excitement and tensions of the past quarter hour.

"Thought you might be," Jaime said. "I saw you come over from the Conejo and turn down the draw yonder. I cut down this way to join you in case you needed a hand. Find what you were looking for?"

Tito shook his head, knowing he'd have to face up to it sooner or later. That was Jaime's way.

"Saw a couple saddled horses in here. Thought it might be drifters, but it wasn't. Just Greta and Quelí. They'd stopped for a swim, I guess. They're up the line a ways, heading for home."

"I know. I saw them leave."

"When'd you get here?"

"Same time you did. Just before they piled out of the creek."

"Look, Jaime," Tito said, "I didn't know what the hell to do. I didn't want to give 'em a start or embarrass them or anything. You know how I feel about Greta. Another sister."

"Not after today, the eyeful you got. You're Spence Stanton's son, and he's a goddam stud. Always has been."

Jaime paused a moment and then continued.

"Funny thing. I almost had my first woman right here. Same damned spot."

"Hell, there wasn't anything like that!" Tito protested—too quickly, he knew.

"I know. Just aim to make sure there ain't going to be. Understand?"

"Honestly, fartherest thing from my mind."

"Bullshit," Jaime said grimly. "I could hear you breathing clean over where I was. His mind ain't what a man puts in a woman when he beds her. You keep yours in your pants around Greta. If she's still at headquarters when you get there, tell her I said she'd better come along home pronto."

Jaime pulled his pony around sharply and started back across the patch of turf. Tito let him go a few yards then called anxiously.

"Jaime, I'd rather you didn't tell her."

"Don't aim to. Just shine her up on a few of the facts of life."

The Missourian rode on.

The yard-boy at the corrals told Tito that Greta Henry had not stopped but had ridden on toward the

Big Cimarron on her way home. He was secretly relieved that he would not have to face her or deliver
Jaime's message.

The boy was rubbing down and walking a heavily
sweated horse from the lower ranch at Mora. He said
Heggie Duncan had just ridden it in. Tito frowned as he
unsaddled his own mount.

Heggie Duncan had once been Spencer Stanton's bit-
ter enemy. However, the huge redheaded Scot had long
been a privileged visitor on the Corona. Headquartered
in Santa Fe, he had in recent years handled the sale of
most of the Corona get through his livestock brokerage
firm and was one of Spence Stanton's closest confidants.

Impetuous as he frequently was, it was not like Heggie to ride a horse as hard as this one had been. The old
Indian trail through the *malpaís* between the Mora and
Corona headquarters was tough enough on saddle stock
with far lighter burdens than Heggie's vast bulk. And he
knew a cardinal rule on both ranches. Hands served the
iron, not individuals. There were no personal servants
on the Corona. Even 'Mana's staff served the household, not its mistress or the members of her family. Every Stanton, from Spence on down to Bronco, looked to
his own gear and stock.

That Heggie Duncan had over-ridden a Corona horse
and had left it in the care of a yard-boy meant that he
was in haste, and when the big man moved that fast,
something important was afoot. Tito turned his pony
into the corral, baited it a small ration of still precious
grain for a day's work well done, and hurried up the
lane toward the house.

The Scottish giant from Santa Fe was in the office
with Spencer Stanton. 'Mana sent Tito in to them without his usual stop at the washbench outside the back
door of the kitchen. As he entered the office he saw at
once that Heggie Duncan was angry. This was not an
unusual state for Heggie, who had about as short a fuse
as a man could light without burning himself. It was

with relief that Tito saw that his father did not seem unduly disturbed.

"What's up?" he asked the two older men.

"Laddie," the fuming Scot rumbled, "ye've been gyved. Gyved and stolen blind!"

"Me?" Tito asked in astonishment.

"Na, na. Wetzel. But it's all the same. It'll be your pocket some day. The gashing gall of the son of a bitch!"

"Simmer down, Heggie," Spence Stanton said. "Here, before you bust a gut."

He shoved the bottle between them toward his guest.

"Somebody held Saul up as he was closing the bank the other night," he said to his son. "Got away with six thousand in gold. Heggie thinks we should call out the militia, at least, if not the whole damned Army of the United States."

"You're no fool for all your stubbornness when you're a mind," Heggie said, splashing his tumbler full of whiskey. "Let a thing like this get started and there'll be no end to it, mon! There's a riffraff of ruffians strung thick as porcupine quills all the way from the Missouri to California these days. Auld Clootie knows we've got our share. And Wetzel wouldn't go to the law—wouldn't even report it!"

"Does anybody have any idea who it was?" Tito asked.

"One man. Inside, anyway. Nobody saw him. Even Wetzel. Ought to have his head blowed off for not sneaking a look at least. I'd a thought a Jew'd be a mon of courage."

Heggie snorted in outrage and drained his brimming tumbler without taking it from his lips.

"Wetzel's right about not reporting it," Spencer Stanton said thoughtfully. "Without identification or witnesses there's nothing to go on. Reporting it would only make it public knowledge. It would only advertise the fact that Corona Trust and Guaranty had been robbed.

Bad for the bank. Bad for us. And nothing accomplished."

"Not sitting here on your duff," Heggie agreed sourly, refilling his tumbler. "That's the bygod truth! Hell, mon, I'm smarting, too. I've got a few shares in that damned bank of yours myself."

"Six thousand dollars isn't going to break any of us."

"Damn it, Spence, you're getting old. Too much lard on your ass."

"I can still bend your arm to the tabletop, you bellering red bastard," Stanton said. "There's more than just a holdup under this bushel. Just one man, apparently. Pretty brassy, right on the plaza. Why six thousand when there had to be closer to fifty in the safe? And he said something to Wetzel about a loan, didn't he?"

Heggie nodded.

"He said to call it that. Making a joke, I'd guess. Rubbing a little salt in on Saul."

"Maybe not. I don't think it was the gold itself he was after. Something he could buy with it—for six thousand dollars. Know anything come up for sale down there at that figure?"

"Not that I can think on."

"It'll come out," Stanton said.

Tito smiled then. He knew his father.

"Then you'll be going to Santa Fe?"

"No," Spencer Stanton said. "That's a damned long ride and maybe a thankless one. It'll likely take some digging to pry this out and I don't have the patience for it. Like Heggie says, maybe I'm getting old. I'm sending you back with him."

Tito was startled but pleased. Santa Fe would be a welcome change from the familiar, daylong monotony of working cattle. And like Heggie, he was outraged at the theft from the bank. It was an affront to the Stanton interests, a challenge to their prestige and influence, and he personally wanted to run down the thief.

"Mind me, boy," his father said, "you find what that yahoo wanted that six thousand dollars for and you'll find him. Move fast enough and maybe you'll find the money, too. If you do, learn him a lesson and turn him over to the law. That's the important thing. The law. We've got to protect it, such as it is way out here, before we can protect ourselves."

"You better pack, laddie," Heggie said, swallowing another prodigious drink. "I want to leave at first light."

Tito started for the door. His father stopped him.

"One other thing. Your half brothers were bound for Santa Fe when they left here. Heggie thinks they didn't stay long if they showed up there or he'd have heard of them or run into them. But they may still be thereabouts. If that should be, you stay clear. The three of you started off with bad blood between you and I want none spilled. It's my own, the same as yours."

Chapter 6

Privately, Blair Stanton did not subscribe to the ready assumption of superiority and leadership that his brother seemed to expect as the birthright of the first-born. In his opinion J.—Neville—was not his equal physically, nor as quick and devious in scheming. He thought his brother's judgments fallible.

But it was easier to let Neville have his way and expend most of the effort. Time enough to make changes or alter stance if it became necessary and opportunity afforded. Such acquiescence cost little if pride was discounted and it made for an easy if deceptive relationship.

Such was the case with the new plan Neville had worked out. Once started it worked with ridiculous ease. For starters, anyway, whatever the final outcome might be. Ted Crane returned that first night from the station at Johnson's Ranch with eleven scrip warrants, each for three hundred and twenty acres of unwatered open government land. He had bought them, he said, from the saddle-mates with whom he had been traveling.

Neville paid him four double-eagles in gold for each. Blair thought the deliberate overpayment too generous in view of the apparent worthlessness of the paper they were buying up. Neville argued that they needed the ex-sergeant's best efforts and could afford to pay for them. They got them.

Crane's sullen, down-at-the-heels attitude vanished as his pockets filled. He spruced himself up and bearded every likely prospect moving along the Trail. As his confidence grew he brooked little argument, even among those who were so disposed or didn't like the price he offered.

At the end of three days they had a stack of seventy-five warrants exchangeable for twenty-four thousand acres of land. Neville thought this would be adequate and it left them a little of the gold he had stolen from Spencer Stanton's bank for their own immediate use.

It would have suited Blair better to have some of the two or three thousand Crane had retained as his cut as well. A fairer division for the services performed. But he let it go. First things first.

When they settled up with Crane for the last of the warrants, the ex-Johnny Blue tried a little sly prying.

"Something up, sure as hell," he said. "You two slicked-up fancy-Dan Rebs holed up here in the brush like squatters and letting me do your hustling. Smart. Nobody's even laid eyes on you, let alone knowing it's you that's buying their scrip."

"Personal preference," Neville told him with a smile. "Always hire anything done you can. Our lily-white hands."

"Manure," Crane snorted. "Three feet deep. Give my eye teeth to know what you're going to do with all that ass-fodder, now you got it."

"Speculation."

"Sure. Never trusted your kind before the war and got less reason to now. Fine fellers like you don't throw away good yaller gold unless they expect to get something a sight more valuable for it. I'd kind of like to know what. The rest of the boys aim to push on. Supposing I stuck around for a spell to find out?"

"Meaning you'd like to stay cut in?" Neville suggested, without humor, now.

"You could say that," Crane agreed, his eyes glinting. "While there's still milk left in the tit, anyways."

"No way," Neville told him tersely. "You've stroked her dry and had your run of luck. More'n you're enti-

tled to. Let it go. Move on. California—Oregon—
wherever."

Blair didn't think the warning was quite blunt
enough. Not with a man like this.

"And keep your goddam mouth shut," he added.
"Shoot it off in Santa Fe and you'll get a visitor you
wouldn't want. I promise that personally. Say a bullet in
the teeth."

Crane looked at him with hardening features.

"Boy," he said harshly, "I been some scared in my
life, but not by no fancy-booted gelding like you. Don't
wave no sticks at me."

He turned and stalked off into the brush toward
Johnson's.

"Good," Neville growled at Blair in disapproval.
"Make an enemy every chance you get. Never know
when you may need one."

"That ignorant, horny-handed bastard? He'd run
from a tail-wagging dog."

"You're going to make a wrong guess one day."

Neville sat down on his grounded saddle with the
sheaf of scrip warrants in his hand.

"We want to keep anybody on the Corona from finding out what we're up to until we're ready for them," he
continued. "People in Santa Fe have seen me. Some may
remember. Particularly in the office where the land records are kept.

"We shouldn't be together, anyway. This damned
hook, too. Always so confoundedly conspicuous. Best I
stay here. Let you go in with these, get them validated
or whatever. Then legally record our title to the land I
showed you on that plat I made. What the hell can the
Corona or its friends do then?"

Blair nodded.

"I was going to propose the same thing," he said.
"Insist on it, in fact. May take a couple days."

"May," Neville agreed. "Whatever's necessary. But
goddamn you, if you lay over to get under a girl's skirt or

drink up the town or do anything to gum this up, I'll hand-whip you to a spot of spit. We've got to do this right and legal the whole way. Spencer Stanton won't allow us one mistake."

"Sure," Blair said.

Let Neville lay down the law again. When he was alone he'd be on his own. There ought to be some fun in Santa Fe. All work and no play . . .

Blair was in the saddle early but as he slanted down from their camp there was already traffic on the Trail below. He pulled up in brush cover and watched a party of ten or eleven Santa Fe-bound men ride briskly past. By their looks and outfits he thought they were the group of drifting ex-soldiers with which Ted Crane had come into Johnson's. However, Crane was not among them.

Curious about this, Blair eased on down to the Trail when the horsemen were well past and gone from view. He spotted Crane then. The former sergeant sat his horse at trailside, talking to the woman who had been in their camp the night that Neville returned from Santa Fe. It appeared that Crane and his companions had met her inbound to morning chores at Johnson's at about the same place Blair himself had first encountered her.

As he watched, Crane dismounted, tethered his horse clear of the Trail, and disappeared into brush there with the woman. Blair smiled. The old Army game and Crane was an old hand. Taking a little of his new gold out in trade where it was afforded before riding on to overtake his companions. Crane didn't know it, but he was being most obliging. He and the woman, both. Blair hoped they took their time. It was a beautiful morning and the grass would be sweet beneath them.

Abandoning his intention to enjoy the good footing and easy wagon-grades of the Trail, Blair reined westward parallel to it, gradually working back up the side-hill he had just descended. When he was high enough above the track to have a considerable view before and behind with little likelihood of chance discovery himself, he pulled up to wait.

It just might become important that no one travelling the Trail see him on it this morning. Neville would approve the forethought if not the rest of it. Small matter. Neville would not have to know.

It was a short ride into Santa Fe and Crane was in no hurry. It was nearly an hour before he reappeared with the woman. She trudged on toward Johnson's. He remounted and jogged on up the pass. Blair let him gain a little lead then rode along parallel and well above.

He slid his rifle from its boot and saw to the cap on its charge. Twice when there was a steep pitch downward to one side of the Trail or the other that he thought suitable for his purpose, he was forced to hold up because of other traffic too near to risk what he had in mind. However, Crane seemed in no hurry to overtake his companions and Blair waited it out.

Finally a third opportunity presented itself near the last ascent of the pass. A sharply cut arroyo cut the Trail here. It was narrow, a scant half a dozen yards, but very straight-walled at this point and thirty or forty feet deep. It was spanned by an unrailed log bridge barely wide enough to accommodate the big freighters now in general use on the Trail.

As Crane approached the bridge, Blair searched the Trail in both directions. He had a considerable stretch of the track in view each way and he thought he could risk it. Swinging down, he sprawled prone behind a small deadfall log convenient as a rest and sighted carefully.

He set the front bead at the crown of the rump of Crane's horse, midway between saddle cantle and tail and followed carefully. When horse and rider were midway across the log span of the bridge and the animal was nervously footing the mistrusted structure, he very gently squeezed off the shot.

The horse squealed and violently kicked hindquarters high at the sting of the bullet. Caught entirely unawares, the rider was pitched sharply forward over the horn, al-most onto the animal's neck, momentarily losing effec-tive control. As the hindquarters of the horse came down one hind hoof missed the outermost log and slashed out in space for support.

The animal threshed valiantly but could not regain its balance and pitched into the ravine, carrying its rider with it. Blair heard the bodies strike the floor. There was no other sound.

Hastily remounting, Blair back-jumped his horse down to the Trail and across it, riding down parallel to the ravine to a break in the near wall that afforded foot access to the bottom. Quitting saddle, he scrambled swiftly down and ran up the floor toward the bridge.

The neck of the horse was broken, the animal dead. He saw that the bullet-crease across the rump would seem but another of the hide-splitting injuries the carcass had received in its fall.

Crane had miraculously managed to kick clear but he lay facedown and inert. Blair rolled him over. One side of his face and head had struck hard against the dry, packed sand of the ravine floor. Blood was oozing from his nostrils and one ear.

Blair did not attempt to discover the extent of other injuries. That was for whatever Samaritan came along directly and discovered the apparent accident. He reached swiftly into Crane's shirt. The worn oilskin pouch was still there. It now clinked heavily with minted coin as Blair lifted it out. He thrust it into his own shirt and sprinted back down the ravine.

Scrambling to his horse on the rim, he rode back to the Trail, eased his mount across the bridge without looking down at the battered bodies beneath, and re-sumed toward Santa Fe, recharging his rifle as he rode. When that task was finished it would no longer make any difference if other travellers met or saw him on the Trail.

What had happened had happened behind him, after he had passed. No one would know. Not Crane. Not

Neville. There was no need. And he had made up for his brother's generosity with the gold from Spencer Stanton's bank.

A few miles further on he encountered the party of ex-Johnny Blues who had passed below him as he was coming down from the camp above Johnson's. They were doubling back, curious that Crane had not overtaken them, and they eyed him narrowly. He waved a friendly, casual greeting and they let him pass without query.

The Federal Land Agent for New Mexico Territory was about as elusive as a virgin in a whorehouse and equally improbable. His office was in a ground-floor cubicle off the cavernous lobby of the old inn called La Fonda. It was locked. The lobby clerk thought it had been for a week or more.

Maybe the agent was on government business in Albuquerque. Or attending to some squabble over Indian lands at one of the down-river pueblos. His duties were many. It could be that he had gone to Trinidad or the district office in Denver. He sometimes did. There was not much business for him in Santa Fe.

Blair eventually found him in a small cantina on a back street where the *aguardiente* was cheap and plentiful. He was a small man with a thin, moth-eaten beard, thick spectacles, and very sad eyes. His name was Rufus J. Smith and the weight of the world was upon his shoulders. He saw the sheaf of scrip warrants and shuddered.

"God help me," he said. "So many? What'd you do, print 'em up yourself?"

"Bought them," Blair answered. "From the men they were issued to. Every one genuine, signed, and witnessed. Seventy-five, all told."

"Lordalmighty, I haven't had that many in the whole Territory since the mustering-out bill was passed. It'll take days. Besides, they're worthless, you know, whatever you paid for them. Or the land you can claim with them is. Mexicans and Indians took up every decent parcel long before we ever got the damned Territory."

"Not the piece I want."

"All them for one piece? Hell, it'd stretch from here to Texas. I'm too busy. See me next week. Monday—yes, I think I'll have a few hours free Monday."

Blair studied the man. He thought he knew what the trouble was.

"How's your job pay?" he asked. "Salary or commissions?"

"Salary?" the little man snorted, aggrieved. "Wages from a government that pays off even its war heroes with worthless shinplasters? You're light in the head, mister. If I could lay hand to the stage fare I'd resign and get to hell out of this goddam country before I'm begging on the streets myself!"

Blair reached into his pocket and brought out a handful of double-eagles. He began to stack them before him, one by one. Rufus Smith watched him with fascination but stopped him on the third.

"No, no!" he said. "I can't accept a commission for redeeming military scrip. It's a free public service. It's against the law to take money."

"From veterans, maybe," Blair said, adding another coin to the stack. "Not from civilians who can afford to pay."

The sad-eyed agent looked at the coins avidly but shook his head with restraint. Blair dropped a fifth gold piece on the stack. Rufus Smith wet his lips and closed his eyes momentarily. He reached into his pocket.

"Your name?" he asked wearily.

"Blair Stanton."

"Well, Mr. Stanton, I just happen to have my seal with me. If the waiter can find pen and ink—"

The required implements were brought. Very rapidly, with fine flourishes of professional penmanship, the agent endorsed the warrants and affixed his seal to each. Blair pushed Neville's plat to him.

"Here's the parcel I want. Twenty-four thousand acres."

"Yes, the warrants will cover that. That's all that matters to me. I've no more time. Take them to the archivist at the Governor's Palace. If the land's open he'll draft you a deed and properly record it. Has to be done in both English and Spanish. He'll send the warrants back to me so I can forward them to Washington."

Blair stood up, pocketed the sheaf of scrip, and pushed the five stacked coins to the agent. He picked them up furtively.

"Stanton," he said thoughtfully. "Big name here. Big ranch, the bank, an interest in Wetzel's store. Very big name."

"In Virginia, too," Blair told him blandly. "Big family. Lot of us."

"No connection?"

"Not that I know of."

"Of course. Coincidence. Happens to me ever now and then. Lot of Smiths, too."

The agent closed his sad eyes again. It was a dismissal. At the door Blair looked back. Rufus Smith already had a fresh bottle of *aguardiente* set before him.

The old man in the recording office in the Governor's Palace counted the sheaf of endorsed warrants, verified the total acreage they represented, and looked at the plat Blair handed him. Seemingly satisfied that all was in order according to the law, he left momentarily.

He returned with a large old hidebound volume of records and began searching out a page. A girl followed him in with an inkstand and some sheets of foolscap. She had a fine, full-lipped face and a soft, busty figure. Blair brightened and put on his best manner.

It gained him nothing. The girl glanced at the warrants the old man handed her and the plat Neville had traced from the records. Only then did she look at Blair, studying him intently. Something in her eyes warned him but he did not understand until her scrutiny strayed from his face down his arm to his right hand.

He had been able to put Rufus Smith off over the coincidence of the Stanton name. The old man here had not seemed to note it as a matter of curiosity or importance. But this girl had at once. And she had remembered an earlier visitor with the same cast of feature.

Neville, the bastard, had not mentioned her. If he had, this could have been avoided somehow or handled in a different way. Perhaps his damned hook had fixed Neville in her mind. The name had done the rest.

Now they were unmasked. They would have to move like hell to get themselves set before Spencer Stanton found out what they were planning. That promise was in those dark, searching eyes.

Blair braced himself for the inevitable challenge but it did not come.

"Rosa will complete your papers for you, *señor*," the old man said. "If you will excuse me . . ."

He left. The girl pulled a sheet of foolscap to her and began to write in a beautiful, unhurried hand. She wrote out another sheet in Spanish and copied both into the big old record book. She folded the two sheets carefully and handed them to Blair with Neville's plat.

"There are you, Mr. Stanton," she said. "Your abstract and a deed from the United States Government. Guard them carefully. They are your evidence of title. I think you will need them soon."

Blair mumbled thanks and left hurriedly. He had a fast ride to make.

Chapter 7

Wetzel was not in the bank nor visible in his store next door. Tito Stanton and Heggie Duncan found him in the little cubicle off the main trade room that served as his quarters. He had a guest. She was seated on the cot, which was the spartan room's chief furnishing.

Rosa Martinez was about midway in age between Quelí Stanton and Greta Henry. She had become a close friend of both when they started coming down to Santa Fe for winter schooling sessions to supplement what 'Mana could offer them at the ranch.

Rosa had a fine, high-boned Mexican beauty and a tantalizing figure Tito privately reckoned second only to Greta's. He flashed her a smile of greeting. She jumped up and gripped his arms earnestly.

"Tito!" she exclaimed with obvious relief, "I'm so glad you're here. But I hoped *Senōr* Duncan would bring your father himself back."

"I'll have to do. You know Spence. Never send a man to do a boy's work. What's up with you two—catch Saul jacking his prices again?"

"I'm afraid this is serious," the girl said gravely. "I'm helping grandpa at the archives, now. A stranger came in a few days ago. A *yanqui,* a little older than you. Nice looking. A gentleman. Wanted to check title to some land up in the north quadrant, over the mountains someplace.

"We were busy on something else so we got him out the folio covering that section and let him find what he wanted himself. He must have. On the way out he asked me to figure what so many *hectáreas* would be in acres.

As I remember it came out to something like twenty-five thousand."

Tito's interest sharpened instantly.

"Before or after you were held up, Saul?" he asked.

"Same day, near as me and Rosie can make out. But the money that was taken wouldn't buy no twenty-five thousand acres of land anywheres that I know of. For cash, anyways. I'd never have seen the connection if Rosie hadn't."

Tito remembered his father's admonition: find what the man who robbed the bank wanted exactly six thousand dollars for and you'd find the thief.

"He show up again—try to register a deed or something?" he asked Rosa.

The girl shook her head.

"But another man did. This morning. Enough like the first to be his brother. The Federal Land Agent sent him to us with a stack of certified scrip warrants and an order to issue an abstract and a federal deed. Tito, the title I recorded and issued was to that big stretch of *malpaís* west of Fire Mountain between your Corona and Mora boundaries."

Tito was astonished.

"What the hell would anyone want to claim that godforsaken ash and lava for? Nobody in his right mind, that's for sure!"

"No it ain't, boy," Wetzel corrected. "Let Rosie finish."

"Somehow I think they're working together and I think maybe it has something to do with you folks," the girl continued. "But what worries me most is that I issued that deed in the same last name as yours. Stanton—a Blair Stanton."

"What?" Tito exploded. "Either one of them have a hook in place of a hand?"

Rosa nodded unhappily.

"The one that came in first. The nice one."

"Nice? Those bastards?" Tito turned to Wetzel. "Heggie knows. My half brothers. Neville and Blair.

Came whining to the ranch, trying to claim a share. Bad-mouthed aplenty when Spence told them where they could go."

"So I began to suspect, the more Rosie told me," Wetzel said with a shrug. "Had to happen, sooner or later, I reckon. Spence has been afraid it might for years."

"You knew about them, too?" Tito asked accusingly.

"That they existed. Not much else. Your pa don't talk much about some things."

Rosa Martinez' eyes were round with astonishment. "Half brothers? I don't understand."

"Long ago and far away," Wetzel said. "What's important's the here and now. All of a sudden there's too damned many Stantons hereabouts."

"Won't be for long," Tito promised grimly. "You delivered that deed to Blair this morning, Rosa. What—five-six hours ago? Not much of a lead when they don't know the country. Anybody have any idea where they might be now—either one of them?"

"One with the deed cleared out in a hurry," Wetzel said. "Where to I don't know. What's the difference if we did? Nothing to be done. We can't prove one of 'em jumped me at the bank, that it was our money they used to buy up that scrip.

"They've got Spence's ranch split in two with that wedge of *malpaís* and they can make it stick. It's as legal a deal as can be had under the law. There's no way of reversing it, now."

Tito touched the butt of his belt-gun.

"The hell there isn't! I've got six easy ways right here, once I've run them down."

Heggie Duncan put out a great, restraining hand and shook Tito's shoulder in dissuasion.

"Na, na, noo!" he protested earnestly. "Na more o' such talk. Ye ken what Spence warned you. For all the reputation ye've won with that gun, it'll go against you. Ye can na use it against your own kith, laddie. 'Twould be—uh—incest!"

The big red Scot seemed vastly pleased the word had come to him so readily.

"Fratricide, technically," Wetzel corrected dryly. "Out and out murder in the eyes of the law. Whatever the circumstances. Very unhealthy in the long run. Besides an indelible stain on the family escutcheon. Heggie's right, boy. Got to be none of that."

The trader shook his head with self-condemnation.

"For all my foxy reputation, I can sure be a dumb bastard. I should have tumbled to what they were up to, if not who they were, when Union drifters started turning up here at the store with hard cash in their jeans instead of the worthless scrip they're always trying to pawn off for beans, bacon, and a bottle."

"A few days—a few hours—would ha' made the difference," Heggie rumbled. "Before they had time to collect enough shinplasters to buy up that deed and record it. But not noo. Auld Clootie take 'em, but they got the lot of us by the short hair, and that's a fact!"

Wetzel shrugged.

"What's done's done," he said.

Tito stirred restlessly. The hell it was!

He had the greatest respect for these two aging friends of his father's. Affection as well. Both bore scars won in defense of the Corona and those upon it. But like Spencer Stanton himself, they were slowing down. Their fires were banked. Caution, logic, and reason were their weapons now. They would accept malicious misfortune at the hands of others rather than strike back as they once had done. The old times, they believed, were dead.

He knew better than to argue further with them or to further reveal his own intentions. Kindly, firmly, even deviously, with the same loyalty to the Stanton brand that once had taken them into battle, they would stop him if they could. For his own good, they would say, and they would believe it.

He shrugged in apparent acceptance.

"Maybe you're right," he conceded. "You usually

are. I reckon the best bet's for me to get back to the ranch on the double and let Spence know what's up before those sons of bitches make their next move. God knows what it'll be but he'll know what to do."

"Aye, noo, laddie, that's Stanton thinking," Heggie Duncan approved with relief. "Spence'll manage something."

"I don't know," Wetzel said. "I don't trust him, either, when somebody tromps his corns a mite hard. I've seen him fly off the handle before. You tell him to keep clear of the law, whatever he does.

"New marshal for the Territory's some ambitious. He's looking for a prime pelt to nail up on his barn door. For show. Make a name for himself. Politics. A big rancher rousting his own sons out of something they come by legally'd do him just dandy. Ain't as many people afraid of Spencer Stanton as used to be. You tell him that."

"He won't believe it but I'll try," Tito promised. He turned to Rosa Martinez. "I'll walk you back across the plaza."

"I'd like that," the girl said with a quick smile. "Give me something to brag about."

She took his arm and they went out across Wetzel's big trade room. However, once into the plaza, Tito steered her down a narrow side street to a little *cocina* in which they could have privacy. They ordered *chocolates* and as Rosa sipped hers Tito spoke to her earnestly.

"I need some help."

"Anything. You know that."

"I remember you have a good horse."

"Ought to be. Spencer Stanton gave it to me."

"Can your granddad spare you for a spell—maybe a week or two?"

"Long as I want. There's always my brother to help."

"Good. Now, didn't Jaime bring you and the girls over El Cumbre one time—the secret old Indian warpass through the high peaks?"

Rosa nodded, brightening at the recollection.

"It's beautiful up there. About the most exciting thing I've ever done. I think we're the only women who've ever crossed it."

"No. Greta's mother was first. When Jaime rescued her after she was kidnapped by renegades and carried off into the Taos valley."

"I didn't know. I've never heard."

"Long time ago, before they were married. Do you remember the way?"

"Every inch. Jaime showed us how to find and recognize the old Indian markers."

"Would you be afraid to tackle it alone?"

"Of course not. The *paisanos* are superstitious about it and it's so high and hard to find nobody else ever uses it. The high peaks are my country, Tito. I never can get enough of them."

"I've got to get word to Spence. You're the best messenger. You've talked to my half brothers. You know the whole story and can answer any questions he asks."

Tito paused and eyed the girl for any sign of reluctance but her eyes were eager.

"Too much riffraff along the freight trail for you to go that way these days," he continued. "And it's the only route north Neville and Blair know. You might run into them and be recognized. I can't let you risk that. God knows what they might do if they realized you were carrying a message to the Corona."

"It's that serious?"

"I don't know. Besides, the wagon road's the long way around. El Cumbre's twice as fast. Time's important. Tell your family you're going to visit friends— whatever—but nobody else. Specially not Heggie and Saul. Slip out of town quietly, as quickly as you can."

"In half an hour, I'll be at the Corona tomorrow night—the next midday at the latest. What do I tell your father about you?"

"That I've disappeared. He'll understand. He'll hear

from me soon enough. Tell him to sit tight until he does."

"Be careful, Tito."

"*Lo mismo.* And thanks, Rosa."

Ringing down a coin and leaving his *chocolate* untouched, Tito left. He had no real concern for the girl. Rosa Martinez was of this country as he was himself. It was not the enemy to them that strangers frequently found it to be. What had to be done she would do and at no risk to herself.

He swung onto his horse in the plaza and rode out past the shuttered tavern in the corner of La Fonda into the narrow cobbled street that was the beginning of the Santa Fe Trail.

On the east slope of Glorieta Pass the descending ruts of the Trail crossed a narrow, deep arroyo on a log bridge. A dead horse lay on the arroyo floor beneath this. The carcass had been stripped of gear but the animal had been killed—apparently by a fall from the bridge—so recently that it was not yet flyblown.

Tito rode on down to the station at Johnson's Ranch. A number of saddled horses were tied at the rack before the common room there. A saddle and tack were tossed over one end of the rail. Tito tied his horse near this and entered the building.

A fat, mixed-blood slattern who had forgotten the pride of her people was tending the wants of a dozen men idling within. All were *extranjeros.* Most wore scattered rags and tags of telltale outworn Union Army issue. One, physically the most prepossessing of the lot, had a massive fresh bruise on one side of his face and head that had swollen his eye shut. He was obviously in pain and in a vicious mood. His companions were hardly more friendly. They eyed Tito with suspicious hostility.

"Which way you men headed?" he asked.

"None of your damned business," one of them said, plainly speaking for all.

"Well, now," Tito said mildly, "if it's plain speaking you want I'll have to disagree with that. Once again: which way you headed? And a decent tongue in your head this time, if you please!"

For all its softness, his voice had the crack of a whip.

The man who had spoken rose lazily to his feet. He looked down at the man with the swollen face.

"Cocky young bastard ain't he, Crane? Needs his manners minded. . . ."

He sauntered toward Tito, unhurriedly reaching for his belt-gun. There was sureness to the movement that, for all its casualness, warned he could use the weapon well. Probably the best of the lot. The knowledge gave him an easy, overbearing confidence. The others watched expectantly as though they had seen him in action before.

Tito read the intent. When the weapon was fully drawn and the gap between them closed, there would be a sudden swipe of the barrel to the side of his head. Perhaps a slash of the foresight to mark his face a little. A dose of pistol-whipping to knock the starch out of him and vent their own sullen mood. Then an unceremonious heave-ho out the door before he could know what was happening. A sure cure for a loose jaw.

Without a shift of balance or a warning flicker of motion in the rest of his easy-standing body, Tito's hand dropped. The butt of his gun smacked smartly into the palm of his hand. Leather whispered softly as the weapon snaked from its holster. The sear clicked to cock and he fired. The whole was an incredibly swift blur of sound perceptible to the ear although the draw was not to the eye.

The bullet struck before the drifter's weapon was even clear of leather. It smashed the gun from the man's grip and tore the holster from his belt. The gun spun to the feet of the man with the swollen face. He saw it coming and was scooping for it as it landed. Tito fired again and the weapon skidded out from under the reaching fingers, coming to rest in the middle of the floor.

All motion in the room abruptly froze, even to breathing. All eyes were on Tito. Incredulity was in them. He dropped his own gun back into its holster.

There was a concerted exhalation.

"Godalmighty!" the man who had tried to draw murmured, absently chafing the numbed fingers of his gunhand.

The man with the swollen face sucked in a great breath and blew it out again slowly.

"Ted Crane," he said in self-introduction, and indicating the others, "My sidekicks. We been hangin' together a spell. Santa Fe bound, if that's what you want to know. California eventually, I reckon."

He glanced at the frightened slattern huddled back against the wall.

"I lagged behind a little when we started out this morning and some son of a bitch dry-gulched me off a bridge up the line a ways afore I could catch up with the boys," he continued darkly. "They got worried and doubled back directly to find me.

"Horse was deader'n a door nail and I was some bunged up, as you can see. Pockets light better'n two thousand dollars, gold, too. This was the closest place to get another broomtail and try to figure out who nailed me. That's the size of it."

"Sounds like you've had yours for one day," Tito said. "I want nothing from you. Except civility."

"Reckon you got it—now," the man named Crane said wryly. "The hard way."

"I'm looking for a couple of fancy-Dan Johnny Rebs. Brothers. One with a hook for a hand. Ought to have been in through here earlier in the day. One anyways."

"Wouldn't mind settin' eyes on them two again myself," Crane said thoughtfully. "They been around a week or more, buyin' up all the musterin'-out land-scrip they could get their hands on. What the hell for I don't know. Boys passed one headin' for Santa Fe when they doubled back to look for me. One with the hook's cleared out, too. We checked the place where their camp was."

"Thanks, Crane," Tito said. "All I need to know."

The man eyed him speculatively.

"Land's all that scrip's good for. Worthless land, at that. Would you have any idea what them two are up to—where they aim to light?"

"No," Tito lied. "Not the foggiest."

"Well, they ain't land-grubbers; I can tell you that. Not by a long shot. I'd kind of like to know what kind of loot they're really after."

"Try Santa Fe. You ought to have that face looked to."

"Might just do that," Crane said. "Mind giving us your handle?"

"Tito Stanton. You'll hear it around."

Tito pulled open the door and stepped back into the sun.

Chapter 8

His half brothers had been trailing packhorses when they rode in to the Corona headquarters and out again. Tito judged they would still be so encumbered. If they were to attempt to take possession of the *malpaís* to which they now held title, they would need more supplies than could be carried behind their saddles. There would be no easy living off the land in that desolate place.

But four horses or two, the sign they left would be little advantage. Traffic north and east of Glorieta Pass was so heavy these days that the tracks of even large parties were obliterated almost as soon as they were made.

The one possible benefit was that Neville and Blair, trailing packhorses, could not make the time a single horseman could. There was the chance that he might not only overhaul them before they got into the wild country up west of Fire Mountain, but slip past them undetected and so be there before them.

As soon as he was out of the confines of Apache Canyon, Tito began short-cutting across the serpentines of the Trail as it clung to longer and easier grades suitable to the heavily laden wagons of the Santa Fe trade. Two hours down toward the meadows at Las Vegas, he found himself on a hogback between two such convolutions.

A compact body of horsemen had appeared behind him, riding no more urgently than he was himself. He recognized the riders at once. They were Ted Crane and the ten or eleven sidekicks who had been with him at

Johnson's Ranch. Presently they left the broad, dusty
track of the Trail as he had done and slanted up the
hogback toward him.

There was no question that they were following him,
trying not to close up but not lagging far enough back to
risk losing him. Tito was not too surprised.

He had known at Johnson's that Crane and his companions had not revealed all they knew of Blair and Neville Stanton. The source, for instance, of the two thousand dollars in gold that Crane had claimed was stolen
from him. Such men did not travel with such a sum.
Not in these days and in this country.

There was the nature of the questions Crane had said
he wanted to ask the brothers, too. And what Crane's
actual intentions were if he could come up with them
again. Plainly he believed it worth his while to ride a
wide detour to accomplish this and he expected Tito to
lead him to the missing men.

Tito supposed his own name played some part in
Crane's determination and he regretted the vanity that
had made him reveal it. That was of minor importance,
now, but he was not pleased with this pursuit.

He believed this would be best handled alone, privately, between himself and his unwanted kin. A personal satisfaction. It was for this reason he had lied to
Saul Wetzel and Heggie Duncan. He had not wanted his
father involved. Or Jaime and the Corona and Mora
crews. Certainly not a pack of shifty and hungry-eyed
drifters looking to line their pockets.

He crossed the ridge of the hogback and started
down the other side, buying himself a few minutes hidden from pursuit and looking for a way to give the slip
to those behind him.

Presently he came to a broad lateral strip of broken
red shale that had spilled from an exposed outcropping
and lay like a bright stripe along the dun side of the
hogback. He automatically started to ride eastward
along this toward lower country, looking for a narrower
place to cross such treacherous footing.

However, after a few moments he changed his mind and took his horse out onto the loose, slatey stone and turned westward along it toward higher ground where the hogback shouldered up into the front ridges of the looming Sangre de Cristos. It was hard, dangerous going and necessarily slow.

Calculating time as closely as he dared, he held to the shale until the last moment, then reined up under the outcropping from which it had fallen. A shoulder thrust out there. It was barely saddle-high but it was the only shelter within reach and he knew it would have to do. He rode behind it, dismounted, and peered over it.

His horse was still snorting nervously in distrust of the bad footing over which they had crossed. He calmed the animal with a reassuring hand. Almost at once Crane and his companions appeared in silhouette on the backbone of the hogback in the shallow saddle through which he had himself crossed. They rode smartly down-slope, studying the country ahead and below, and reached the belt of broken shale about two hundred yards distant from and slightly below the level of the rock sheltering Tito and his horse.

They pulled up sharply there, mistrusting the footing as he had. Beyond the shale, further downslope, were scattered copses of thicket-brush, several large enough to conceal a horse and rider. Eastward in the direction in which Tito had at first started, there were a few more scattered thickets of similar size on both sides of the stripe of broken red stone.

There was a brief consultation and it was the latter direction they took, paralleling the belt of shale and angling further downslope with it, looking for a narrower place to cross it as he had intended to do. Their eyes did not lift toward his position at all, so his scant cover remained adequate.

Tito grinned with satisfaction. The trick he had employed was an old one in the mountains. He had learned it from Chato of the Utes when he was a boy and Chato's people still wintered just within the canyon

of the Cimarron. Chato thought that it was a characteristic of people who travelled the mountains by horse-
back. He claimed most horsemen and their mounts
would instinctively choose a downgrade over a climb of
even short duration, and so assumed others would do
the same. Tito doubted this. Even game could be suc-
cessfully stalked in the same way—from above. He believed it had something to do with the nature of the eye.

At any rate, almost invariably at a high place, the
attention of man or beast scanned what lay below with
scant interest in what lay above. The almost sole excep-
tions were the bighorn sheep and mountain goats—
probably because they habitually placed themselves on
the highest vantage available in the first place.

As Crane's party disappeared into the first of the
thickets on east, Tito remounted and climbed on west
along the stripe of shale banding this side of the hogback. Twice they reappeared in open patches, still angling downslope and now cutting widely in search of
some sign of his passage. The second time the distance
and difference in altitude had increased so much that he
did not try to find shelter but continued climbing on
toward the shoulders of the mountains.

In half an hour Crane and his companions recognized
that he had somehow given them the slip. They
bunched again and turned due eastward toward the
gray-green loom of the grasslands and the broad scar of
the Santa Fe Trail occasionally visible there. Tito swung
north himself then, holding well up on the slope of the
frontal foothills until in the late twilight he had the de-
tached, truncated cone of Fire Mountain in view.

A rill came down from above and he followed it into
a tiny hanging meadow lost in timber. The grass was
good and he was weary. He stripped and hobbled his
horse and built a fire to make a mug of coffee with
which to wash down a cold supper from his saddlebags.
In twenty minutes he was asleep while the mountains
whispered around him.

Tito's Indian alarm clock awakened him promptly at midnight, a simple matter of drinking enough water before turning in ensured this. The moon was high on the eastern face of the range and bright enough to throw a shadow as he moved. He broke camp, saddled, and rode on by its light.

Although there was no likelihood of a chance encounter with Abelardo or one of the *vaqueros* stationed there at this hour of the night, he stayed high enough on the flank of the Sangre de Cristos to have timber shelter until he had bypassed the Mora ranch completely.

It was well after daylight when he intersected the thin, overgrown trail that descended the eastern side of the formidable, seldom-used old Indian pass over El Cumbre. Although he doubted any possibility that Rosa Martinez could have yet made it this far, he rode along the track for a quarter of a mile or so in search of recent sign.

There was none. Rosa was still up there in the great, chill peaks somewhere. He was relieved. He had been afraid that in her earnest desire to help, she might have been tempted to continue her climb after she lost her light. As far as he knew, only two reckless and skillful men had ever crossed the great pass at night and alone—Spencer Stanton and Jaime Henry.

Thereafter he rode due east out of the green and welcoming mountains toward the stark, volcanic loom of Fire Mountain and into the *malpaís*. It was a sere and friendless place, a hell gone cold and hard, with a brooding mood of hostility that had always gone athwart Tito's nature. It was a place of ancient death with a brittle hostility to all living things.

As the ash and basalt and obsidian thickened and the farspreading dikes built up, Tito's horse became more and more restive and reluctant to go on. It was almost as though the animal sensed the enmity of the burned-out land. However, Tito understood the real difficulty.

Dismounting and transferring the remaining contents of his saddlebags to his bedroll at his cantle, he cut the bags into four sheets of tough, thick leather and some lashing-thongs. With these he shod his horse over its iron shoes. Thereafter the animal proceeded without further protest.

Unshod cattle, storm-driven or perversely drifting into the fringes of the *malpaís,* lamed very quickly and soon were downed, unable to rise again. The razor-sharp shards of obsidian, fractured from the molten surface in cooling, littered the footing everywhere and gouged out the sole and frog of unprotected hoofs as easily as did a farrier's knife.

There were smooth surfaces in the *malpaís,* flows that had been swept clean by wind and storm or that had not cooled so fast as to fracture, but they were few and far between and a man rode many tortuous extra miles to travel by them. Tito had no time or patience for that.

He knew the clumsy, makeshift boots he had fashioned for his horse would last no great distance but it was of no matter. He knew precisely where he was going. The way was not far. He could afford to hold on in a direct line.

There were scattered grass pockets in the *malpaís,* watered in season by snow, rain, and runoff, where the volcanic overburden had weathered and broken down into a soil of sorts that would reluctantly accept seeding by the wind again. Tito did not know how many of these there actually were.

He supposed no man did. Or the area they totalled in the aggregate. Perhaps a thousand acres out of the many thousands his half brothers had bought up with stolen Stanton gold and their worthless scrip.

But in all the vast expanse from the foot of Fire Mountain to the foothills of the Sangre de Cristos, there was only one known permanent source of water. This was a deep, spring-fed pool in one of the scattered pockets of grass. It neither overflowed nor changed its level from season to season.

This was his destination. Rosa Martinez had said Neville and Blair had secured a copy of a plat of their purchase from the archives in Santa Fe. This water would show upon it. They would know its importance to their survival. It would be their destination as well. And when they arrived, he would be waiting for them.

Neville Stanton was not prepared for the brutal reality of the *malpaís*. Such tortured country could not be imagined from a casual distance. He felt a growing stir of misgiving concerning the course that he and his brother had committed themselves.

Blair had retained the other documents they had secured in Santa Fe but Neville rode with the plat of their purchase open across his thigh. Water was indicated at only one place between Fire Mountain and the Sangre de Cristos. Nowhere was there indication of shelter or source of supplies beyond those they carried in their packs. Always excepting, of course, the hostile headquarters of the two Stanton ranches.

Such geography left them with a slender base of operations. Still, if a man selected a sound position in the eyes of fair men and saw to it that it had the sanction of law, he could risk locking horns with a formidable opposition and have some hope of prevailing to a reasonable degree. Even against as powerful and high-handed an adversary as Spencer Stanton.

In essence this was the gamble—the game—that all men of business played, plotting against each other for the ultimate advantage. That was how Neville had planned that he and Blair would plot against their father. Both understood such tactics. It was the heritage of their kind, the wages of the way they had been raised, and they had their skill at it.

By these qualifications and the accepted rules of such games—such gambles—the odds seemed fair enough. If they stood firmly by their intent and refused to be intimidated, a satisfactory accommodation should be reached in time, no matter how stubborn and arrogant the foe.

But Neville now realized that they had not reckoned on the possibility of the country itself becoming another adversary beyond the force of law and human covenant. He sensed that this *malpaís* might prove to be just that—impervious to man-made rules, immutable, and unforgiving.

This vague foreboding continued to grow as they rode deeper into these basalt barrens. There obviously were good and ample reasons why others in the past had not put their mark on this desolation before them.

For generations Virginians had broken and tamed their land according to the scope of their ambitions and their skill in connivery and competition. But this was a country that could break men and tame them.

He and Blair had the ambition, God knew, and were skilled enough in connivery to have their way this far. But he wondered if they had the flint to match this glassy, growthless rock.

Neville watched his brother covertly, seeking some reflection of his own thoughts. However, Blair seemed undisturbed by their surroundings. He glanced occasionally behind them, but he seemed as disinterested in where they had been as in their eventual destination.

He seemed content enough to let Neville try to pick their way from the plat he kept ready for reference. The tortuous route they followed and the fetlock-deep ash and windrows of laming chip obsidian they frequently had to cross could have been a bluegrass-turfed Virginia lane for all the concern he showed.

It was almost as though Blair was buoyed by some inner confidence in the ultimate outcome of their scheme, a sureness of the progress of coming events, and a foreknowledge of the means to achieve them. Neville supposed it sprung from some subtle difference in their natures, but that conclusion was no comfort to his own unease.

It was the fourth day since they had slipped away from the camp above Johnson's Ranch. They had dry-bedded the night before on a little patch of unwatered grass, surrounded by the awesome silence of the lifeless *malpaís*.

Starting again before dawn, they had ridden out half of the afternoon. Neville still had no real notion of where the waterhole they were seeking might be among the unfamiliar and confusing landmarks tumbled about them. He was beginning to have real concern for their waterless stock.

Blair still occasionally glanced disinterestedly behind them as he did elsewhere about the frustrating and monotonous terrain, but he remained untroubled. After half an hour of silence, he spoke.

"When you pick a place to hole up, you sure pick it," he said, pulling up. "About as far from the niceties of civilization as you can damn well get. Suppose the boat'll wait?"

He slid down and handed Neville his reins and packhorse lead.

"Got a call to make."

He crunched away across the eternal rubble underfoot and disappeared around the tongue of a lava dike nearby. Neville thought the modesty curious. Blair was not one to waste unnecessary effort. He would as soon pee from the saddle as dismount. Neville waited impatiently, aware of the lowering sun.

Presently there was a startling sound in this silent place, the ring of a steel shoe on glassy rock. It was followed by other sounds of approach. Neville twisted in his saddle. Ted Crane rode from behind another lava dike at the head of the ragtag company of discharged Johnny Blues that he had been travelling with when they first encountered him.

Encumbered by all four horses, Neville sat motionless in his saddle. It was a wise judgment. There were several drawn guns in Crane's bunch. All were covering him. And there was unmistakable hostility in the ex-sergeant's manner as they rode up to him.

"Where's your brother?" Crane demanded without preface.

"Yonder," Neville said with a tilt of his head in the direction Blair had taken. "Call of nature."

"Yeah?" Crane growled suspiciously. "Finicky, ain't he? We'll see. 'Light down, real easy."

Neville stepped down carefully. Crane and his companions also dismounted. Some took charge of the horses. Crane lifted the gun from Neville's belt, ramming it into his back.

"In case your brother tries something foolish. Move!"

Chapter 9

With Crane pressing his own gun into his back and two of the others following them, Neville led off toward where Blair had disappeared. They rounded the tip of the dike. A few yards away Blair was squatted down, pants about his heels, on a pocket of obsidian chips. Behind him was a heap of dung where he had relieved himself. He seemed genuinely startled.

"Where the hell did you come from?"

"The Trail, same as you," Crane said. "Followed you in. Bitch of a job, too. You seen us. Had to. Either keep that close or take a chance of losing you, and we didn't aim to do that, mister."

Blair glanced at Neville and shook his head.

"Never even thought of anybody behind us. Not in this devil's rockpile. Did we?"

"No," Neville said, answering honestly for himself. Crane shrugged.

"Let it go," he told Blair. "Cob your ass and come on."

Blair hauled up his pants and stuffed in the tail of his shirt. He had put his belted gun aside for convenience. Crane scooped it up and gestured them back toward their horses. They obeyed. As they rejoined the rest of Crane's crew the ex-sergeant barked an order to his men.

"Strip the bastards and search them packs."

Hands lay hold of them. In moments they were buff naked. Each garment was gone through meticulously. Their packs were pulled down, spread open, and each item of their contents was thoroughly gone over.

Directly, Crane's men had brought him the plat Neville had been carrying, the other documents Blair had picked up in Santa Fe, and the few loose coins that were the last of their gold. Nothing else.

Slow anger built in Neville Stanton. He could see no reason for this high-handed search. He wanted no more of this riffraff. The bastards had served their purpose and he didn't like the interest Crane was displaying in the plat and the title documents from Santa Fe. But they were helpless against such odds. It further irritated him that Blair did not seem unduly disturbed.

"Give 'em their clothes and make up the packs again," Crane ordered. "Suppose you two figure you got an apology comin'. Well, you don't. Ain't my nature."

He watched Neville and Blair as they redressed. He seemed amused by their predicament but he attempted some amends in spite of his denial.

"Fact is I got bushwhacked for my share of the gold you paid me. Better'n two thousand dollars that was going to give me and the boys a lift on toward California. Nigh got kilt, to boot."

He returned their guns.

"Such like makes a man some hostile," he continued. "You two knew I had them yellow eagles. You give us the slip at Johnson's. I figured if you'd got it you'd have it on you. Just had to know. That's all."

"Makes sense," Blair agreed without resentment. "But there's politer ways of finding out."

"Told you it ain't my nature."

Neville eyed the documents Crane still held.

"I'll take those."

"Sure," Crane assented. "Interesting, ain't they? I couldn't figure you two and all that scrip. Plain enough, now. Balls. I fancy that. Workin' out just right. You're going to need some hard-nosed hands. We're fresh flat-assed broke again and lookin' for hire."

"We go this alone," Neville said.

"Balls, maybe, but no brains," Crane snorted scornfully. "The two of you against the biggest man in the Territory and the crew of the biggest ranch? Horsecock! That's like usin' a full powderkeg for a thundermug with a lighted cigar between your teeth."

"Strictly a family matter," Neville answered sharply. "Old Man Stanton's our father."

"So's godalmighty, so the preachers claim, but that don't keep the good Lord from visitin' hellfire and damnation on a man and gettin' hisself damn well kilt to boot if he ain't careful."

"We'll manage."

"In a pig's eye! You're bare-assed babes when it comes to somethin' like this. And you ain't the only Stantons headed up this way from Santa Fe. Another showed up at Johnson's soon after you cleared out. Not much more'n a kid, but honest to God whelped to this country. Fastest hand with a gun I ever seen. Ask ol' Zep, over there. Damn near lost a hand for a little hoorawin'. And he was lookin' for you two."

For the first time Blair showed quick concern.

"Roberto—Tito?" he asked.

"Some such name," Crane agreed complacently. "We tried tailin' him, thinking he might lead us to you, but he give us the slip a couple days back. He's in here ahead of you someplace. He'll be waitin' or I'll miss my guess and take it from me, he could handle a dozen like you with no one left to tell what happened or where the carcasses lie."

"I told you," Neville said impatiently. "We don't need you and we don't want you, Crane. Any part of you."

"Well, now," the ex-sergeant said, eyeing his companions. "Maybe I can't count, but the way I see it, you ain't got much choice."

"He's right," Blair cut in. "We're bucking enough as it is. And they could come in mighty handy. What do you want, Crane?"

"Wages. Whatever's fair. Sure as hell nothing out here we want, whatever you're after. Enough loot to get

us on to California. Cash. If you can get anything out of
your kin, you can get enough to do us. Say whatever we
earn and let it go at that."

"If I told you to go to hell?" Neville said.

Crane smiled benignly.

"Reckon we'd have to change your mind. For your
own good."

Neville looked to Blair for backing. There was none.

"Suck in your gut," Blair told him. "This suits me a
hell of a lot better. Why lone-hand it if we don't have
to? If the old man or his whelp gets nasty, we can trade
'em in kind."

"Good," Crane said, assuming Neville's compliance
as well. "First thing's to jerk the fangs out'n that young
rooster that braced us at Johnson's. We got to find water. When we do, we'll find him. Leave that to me."

Blair gestured toward Neville.

"Want the map to go by?"

"Don't trust maps much," Crane said. "Specially
handdrawn ones like that. One man's rod's another's
mile when it comes to puttin' rough country on paper.
But you can't fool thirsty stock. Give 'em their heads
and you'll see. Let's get movin'."

"Go ahead," Blair said. "You interrupted something.
I can't sit a comfortable saddle till I've finished. Be up
with you directly."

He started off with his led horse toward the dike
beyond where they had found him. Crane chuckled and
led out. Neville found a discharged Johnny Blue on
each side of him and their looks were plain. He followed Crane and the others brought up the rear.

True to his intent, Crane let his reins lie slack on the
neck of his mount. Uncertain for a moment over this
lack of restraint, the animal hesitated. Then it began to
step out, picking footing carefully and taking a course
slightly to the south of that Neville had been choosing
for Blair and himself. Crane looked at him mockingly.

In about five minutes Blair overtook them and rode
confidently past the others to ride stirrup beside Ted

Crane. As he passed, Neville saw that his brother's near boot had a small, ash-encrusted smear of fresh dung on the edge of its sole. He frowned curiously. Blair was fastidious and usually more careful where he stepped.

At some time in the past—Tito did not remember exactly when—some relatives of the Bacas and other *vaqueros* at the Mora ranch had squatted on the springs at Ojos Negros. Unable to find employment at Mora or the Corona, they had surreptitiously slipped into the *malpaís,* apparently intending to exercise squatter's rights and graze sheep on the scattered grass pockets.

The attempt was a failure and they would have starved had Spencer Stanton not moved them to a bunch-grass bench north of Fire Mountain where they and their children yet ran a few flocks at a token rental of a few head of table-lamb each year. But during their tenure at Ojos Negros they had walled off the main spring from their stock to protect their own water supply and had built three stout but crude *jacals* of lava rock and rubble.

Later, before Spence had given up the station contracts at the Corona and Mora and had closed both ranches to the stage line south from Willow Springs to Santa Fe, the route had been bent from the old Indian trail it otherwise followed between the Corona and Mora to provide a water-stop at Ojos Negros. Some other improvements had been made at the springs at that time.

The structures were still there, walls intact and overshadowed by a huge cottonwood from which Spencer Stanton had once found a dead man swinging by his neck in the wind, but they had been long abandoned. Tito supposed he was the first member of either crew who had ridden this far into the *malpaís* in several seasons. If he had his way he'd be the last as well.

The water at the main spring was still good. He unsaddled his horse outside the protective wall and hazed it off toward the lesser springs pocked into the grassed convolutions stretching off into the twisted lava. With some satisfaction he saw the animal presently disappear. There was no need to unnecessarily advertise his presence. Surprise was always an advantage in any such meeting as he now anticipated.

He carried his gear into one of the *jacals*. The sodded roof was sound. By *paisano* standards it was still habitable. Standing as it did in the shade of the big cottonwood, the interior was cool after the reflected heat of the open *malpaís*. He stretched his blanket before his saddle and sprawled supine against it to regain the sleep he had lost in the night.

Strangely, sleep would not come. The obstinacy irritated Tito. Like his father, he could not abide waiting upon the whims and intents of others. Both of them lacked 'Mana's patience, the eternal calm of this unhurried land. Like Spence, Tito expected his body to do his mind's bidding, at once and with ease. To sleep was better than to wait. At least the time was not wasted.

He supposed his restlessness had some root in his subconscious, but he could find no cause and was further annoyed. He wanted this over and done with.

Afternoon shadows lengthened swiftly toward twilight. Tito's nameless irritation increased. He had hoped his timing was about right. Neville and Blair Stanton would be in some hurry, anxious to see firsthand what they had acquired and just how well it was actually suited to their purpose. Discounting their inexperience with the high country, they should have had time now to make it up from Johnson's with the aid of their map by way of the Santa Fe Trail.

However, it was beginning to appear that he would have to wait out the night here in expectation that they would show tomorrow. He would rather have settled with them at once, whatever that might entail, and have gone on into the Corona before nightfall, the job done and the threat permanently scotched. That was the Stanton way as he knew it. That was what Spence would expect.

Nevertheless, he continued to listen idly for the careless sounds of approach that outlanders were certain to make in the windless silence of the *malpaís*. There were none, yet suddenly the doorway of the *jacal* was darkened. For an instant Tito thought his horse might have drifted back, but he knew he would have heard the animal.

He surged to his feet, gun in hand. A voice warned sharply from the darkened doorway.

"I wouldn't, Stanton. Too many of us."

The flat, hard tone was vaguely familiar. Another voice beyond the doorway cut in.

"Let him try. Got to, sooner or later, if I have my way."

There was no mistaking Blair Stanton's soft, almost affected Virginia accent and dispassionate malice.

The silhouettes blocking the light in the doorway moved cautiously into the single room, warily spreading out. As exterior light fell on their faces Tito recognized Ted Crane and four of the long-riders who had been with him at Johnson's. Their hands were full, the muzzles of their weapons unwaveringly focused on him.

He saw with wry disdain that Blair Stanton had prudently remained outside, out of line of sight and fire. Doubtless the other half brother and the rest of Crane's bunch were there with him. It made long odds. Too long under the circumstances.

"The gun, Stanton," Crane said. "Or have it where you stand."

Tito hesitated, then started to drop his weapon into its holster.

"No," Crane objected. "Once is enough with you. Might as well be in your hand as your belt, the way you move. Here."

He scuffed his toe in the pumice of the floor at his feet.

Tito understood at once what had happened. He cursed his own confidence at the belt of shale on the hogback above the Trail where he had so easily given these men the slip. When they lost him they had simply descended to the eastward grass and the Trail again, and had fallen in with or overtaken his half brothers there.

Some kind of a deal had been made between them. Crane, animal-wise and wary, had dismounted them at a distance, coming in silently afoot across the grass flooring of the pocket at Ojos Negros. What Tito had intended to be a simple, private matter between three mismatched Stantons had become complex and infinitely more difficult to manage.

Shrugging, Tito slowly reversed the gun in his hand and tossed it at Crane's feet. One of the Johnny Blues scooped it up. Seeing this from outside, Blair Stanton and another Crane man entered the *jacal*. No others were with them.

His half brother stopped before Tito, satisfaction in his eyes.

"One for me and one for Neville," he said. "Brotherly love."

He glanced at the two nearest of Crane's men.

"Hold him."

The man whose gun he had shot away at Johnson's and another seized Tito's arms, trussing them back. Blair stepped in quickly, ramming one knee brutally up under Tito's belly. Pain drove the wind from him and he sagged forward involuntarily. Before he could recover, Blair swung twice, once with each hand. Each was an unhurried, measured smash up into Tito's face with the full weight of Blair's body behind it.

The room spun. Tito's knees buckled and he hung limply from his trussed arms. Through a fog of fury and the roar of blood in his head he heard his half brother calmly explain to Crane and the rest.

"Payment in kind. Did the same to my brother and me."

Crane spoke from somewhere in the reeling room.

"With your arms behind your back? Like hell.

You're a dumb shit, Stanton. This don't make what you aim to do here no easier. And it won't make your brother too damn proud. It don't me, neither. Turn him loose, Zep."

Hands freed Tito's arms. He staggered back, stumbled across his saddle, and sank onto it with his head between his hands, waiting for it to clear.

"Keep your goddamn opinions to yourself, Crane," Blair snapped. "I don't give a hoot in hell what you think. Or Neville, either. We're up against a hard man in Spencer Stanton. The only way's to hit him hard, every chance we get, and to keep on hitting till he comes to his senses or has had enough. The harder and sooner the better."

"It's your hide, bucko," Crane's voice answered. "Fry it if you want. But now you've started her, you got to move fast. This one come straight here without tryin' to get to the ranch. That means one thing. He sent a message to your old man from Santa Fe. Likely on the old stage road that goes up through Mora, according to your map.

"If that message has got through, we're for sure between a rock and a hard place that ain't going to get any softer an' time's awastin'. Block that trail and we'll at least have some warning. We're lordy damn well goin' to need it, mister!"

"As soon as Neville and the other half of your bunch gets in from that circle you sent them on," Blair agreed. "You and your boys can handle it."

"Not me," Crane said. "Not till I know a hell of a lot more about what we're up against. And I've talked some more to this one and your brother. Some things you can't hire from the black-balled devil hisself. Deliberate damn foolishness is one."

"You expect me to block that old stage road by myself?"

"Unh-uh," Crane answered. "Just put your neck where your mouth an' your damn bloody knuckles are. Take what boys is here. They can take care of theirselves. Zep and I can do here till your brother comes in with the rest."

"You'll back us up if we run into something and need it?"

"Time to decide if you do. Want to be a rich man, get movin'. And watch you don't lame your horses. Damn poor country to be afoot in. Specially if you're bein' hunted."

"All right," Blair said. "Let's go, boys."

Tito opened his eyes and watched them go, as silently as they came. Presently, when they had retrieved their horses from where they had left them, he heard them ride toward the foot of the mountains and the road from the Corona to Mora. He saw that Crane was watching him.

"If that son of a bitch is as hard and smart as he is mean, we just might get along," the renegade said.

Chapter 10

Zep took up a station at the door. Crane went outside, to watch Blair's departure Tito assumed. When the renegade returned he carried a bandanna dripping with water from the spring. He tossed it to Tito.

"You're some messed up. Swab down and you'll feel better."

Tito wiped the blood from his face and cooled the bruised flesh where his half brother's blows had landed. The hard knot of agonized flesh that had popped up in his groin had eased and smoothed. Fortunately Blair's knee had been a little off target.

When Tito was finished Crane moved over and squatted near him.

"So's you know, Stanton, I figgered your brothers might a been the ones that lifted my poke, since I got it in pay from them and they knew I had it. That's why I trailed you, thinkin' you'd lead us to 'em. See now I should a known better. So when we picked 'em up, we followed 'em. Me an' the boys set a store by that gold. But we shook 'em down good out yonder a way an' they didn't have it."

"I'm surprised," Tito growled. "Like 'em. That damned Blair, anyway."

"Yeah, well, some is thieves and some is worse," Crane said. "Me, my wants is simple. I don't give a damn about this country except to get out of it. Neither do the rest of the boys. Get that straight. We don't give a damn about your quarrel or your old man's ranch. We've got to get us a kitty again, the quicker an' fatter the better."

"You horse-trading, Crane?"

"Might say. Sometimes a feller comes out right good that way. I got a pretty good idea of what your brothers is after. Gives me a fair notion of what me an' the boys might be worth to 'em if we help make it stick."

"No way, mister."

Crane shrugged.

"Not easy, maybe. What is? But it comes up we need a mite more help, it can be had. Plenty of empty pockets, flat bellies, and belted guns along the Trail these days. And nobody fussy. Depends on how much geld can be had."

"Highest bidder, eh?"

"Can't say it plainer. We'd whore all comers for a clean shot at California or the Northwest."

Shrewd devils danced in Crane's eyes.

"You're a businessman, Stanton, or should be. And your old man sure as hell is. Forget the short hair. We ain't goin' to yank less'n we have to. Just say we'd admire to know what it'd be worth to you an' your old man to get shut of us without barkin' no shins. Rid of your brothers, too, at the same time, far as that goes—if the price is right."

"We've had our share of rotten bastards stray onto the Corona, Crane," Tito said in his mother's deceptively soft voice. "Mora, too. Couple on the fringes of the family, right now. If you haven't found that out yet you will. But we've never bought a dead man nor paid a dime to one who didn't earn it with the same sweat the ranch has cost us all from the beginning."

"Fair warning?"

"Fair as you're entitled to. Whatever the papers my half brothers got in Santa Fe, this is Corona country. There isn't a man alive who can stand against me or even my little brother, let alone Spencer Stanton and the men who ride for his iron. Especially here in the *malpaís*."

Crane picked up his damp bandanna where Tito had draped it over the horn of his saddle. He balled it up in his palm, compressing his fist so that the last of the moisture trickled from it.

"Fair is as fair does," he said imperturbably. "Seemed you was due your chance. This is the last hand I'll lend you, come hell or high water. Maybe it'll wind up me an' you. Maybe it won't. But from here on you're on one side of the tree and me the other. Don't forget it!"

He rose, stuffed the limp bandanna into his pocket, and went outside.

Less than fifteen minutes after Blair Stanton pulled out with some of Crane's men to blockade the only passable road between the Corona headquarters and the lower ranch at Mora, another party of horsemen rode warily up to the lava wall surrounding the *jacals* and the main spring at Ojos Negros. Zep left the doorway and disappeared into the yard. Tito crossed to the door and looked out.

The riders were his other half brother and the balance of Crane's companions. They dismounted and climbed over the poles closing the gate in the enclosure walls. Crane and Zep met them as they gratefully knelt to water at the spring. Their voices came clearly across the yard.

"Drew a dead end the way you sent us," Neville complained to Crane. "Had to double back a hell of a ways. Took us forever to find another way in. Saw nothing. Not a sign."

"Some has the luck," Crane said.

"How about you?" Neville asked anxiously. "Anything here?"

"The jackpot."

Crane indicated the doorway of the *jacal* where Tito stood. Neville stiffened instinctively as he saw Tito. Crane laughed at him.

"Don't worry. I drew his teeth."

The ex-soldier tapped the butt of Tito's gun, which he had thrust under his own belt. "Your brother worked him over a little for good measure, too."

"Where's Blair and the rest?" Neville asked sharply.

"This is a workin' outfit. No weeds under our ass. They rode yonder to cut the trail between the Corona and Mora."

"Trouble there already?"

"Not yet. But ought to be, directly. What you wanted, ain't it—chop the ranch in two? Didn't see no reason for wastin' time with the cards comin' our way."

"They know at the Corona and Mora?"

Crane shrugged.

"That's what we aim to find out." He indicated Tito again. "Got no word from him, anyways. He come straight here."

"You sure?"

"He'd a had to. Deliberately, I'd say. Been here for hours. Sleepin' when we pussyfooted up on him."

"Damn it, that doesn't make sense. Got to be a reason. Come on. Rest of you turn out the horses."

Tito watched Neville and Crane approach but said nothing when they reached him. His half brother also remained silent, searching him warily with his eyes. After a long moment Neville turned to Crane.

"Give him his gun," he ordered.

Crane's jaw slackened in astonishment.

"You out of your goddam head?" he protested.

"I know what I'm doing. Matter of gentlemen. Give him his gun."

"I told you I seen him work," Crane warned. "Faster'n hell an' tricky as a stomped snake in tall grass."

"That's an order, Crane."

Crane reluctantly passed the gun across.

Those who had come in with Neville had clambered back over the wall and were unsaddling their thirsty mounts, freeing them to seek grass and one of the lesser springs in the pocket. However, Tito saw that Zep remained at the main spring, alert and wary, closely watching the trio before the *jacal*. He took the proffered weapon and holstered it without comment.

Neville indicated his bruised features.

"Blair?"

"Wouldn't a tried it if I hadn't had this bucko's gun an' two stout hands cinchin' his arms back so's he couldn't move," Crane said.

"I'm sorry about that, Robert—" Neville began in a conciliatory tone.

"Tito."

"All right," Neville corrected impatiently. "Tito. That's not my way. Better a fair start between reasonable men. Agreed?"

"Start's already been made."

"Not too late."

"Was for you before you ever rode onto the Corona."

"Right's with Blair and me and you know it. You've been to Santa Fe. You found out what we were able to do there. All legal, right down the line. Spencer Stanton can buck us. Maybe bend us some if he's of a mind. But he can't break us. Not against the law. Not when we're defending our legal rights."

Tito shook his head.

"For a smart-talkin' jasper you don't learn worth a damn," he said. "Any *paisano* kid on the grass'll tell you: Spence makes his own law up here."

Tito saw heat rising in his half brother as his impatience grew.

"Hogwash! Once maybe. No more. He tries, the territorial government'll have to make an example of him. It has no other choice. In the long run it'll cost him—all of you, for that matter—a hell of a lot more than the fair and modest share Blair and I are entitled to for the name we bear."

"He'll try just the same, if you push him. And he'll make it stick. It's a habit he's got."

"Christ, man, we've got the same blood," Neville protested. "The same father, anyway. Least you can do is go to him, show him how it is, try to argue some common sense into him."

Tito shook his head again.

"Old saying hereabouts: 'Does a priest try to argue with God?' I know my place. You'll learn yours."

Neville Stanton irritably clicked the gripping claw on his hook.

"I warn you, Crane and his men are with us if we say so."

"Are anyway, whether you do or not," Crane corrected.

Neville shot him a dark look but ignored the interjection.

"We can get plenty more. All we need. And the Corona will pay their wages in the end."

Tito eyed his half brother levelly. He knew the threat was not empty and he knew the odds in a pitched battle. With the best of planning too much was left to chance in such a confrontation. Most of all there was his father. If these bastards by his first wife riled him too much, a pitched battle would be Spence's way.

He had not planned on Crane and his men and he regretted he had sent a message to the Corona. What Spencer Stanton didn't know couldn't hurt him for the time being.

"Well," he said with outward calm, "maybe these Johnny Blues you're bragging about managed to win themselves a war a spell back, but this one they won't. They don't know what fighting's about till they've tangled with the Corona."

"Suppose we wait and see," Ted Crane said, matching his tone mockingly. He indicated Neville Stanton. "To keep things on the safe side, you better give the man back your gun."

Out of the corner of his eye Tito saw the man called Zep stiffen beside the spring. Then Zep eased his gun out and held it ready.

Shrugging philosophically and seemingly unhurried, Tito took one short step toward Neville, putting Crane between himself and the man at the spring. In that same easy movement his gun came into his hand at full cock, its muzzle scant inches from the buckle of Neville Stanton's belt.

He let the weapon hold steady there for an instant, then he eased the hammer down, reversed his grip, and extended it to his half brother butt-first.

"So you get the notion," he said.

Neville stared at the weapon, then slowly reached out with his hook. Steel rasped against the brass frame. The claw closed and the gun was lifted from Tito's hand.

Zep hurried up angrily, thrusting his weapon before him. Crane gripped Tito's shoulder and propelled him into the doorway of the *jacal*.

"Get in there and stay put!" he ordered. "So much as show your head again and you'll have a bullet hole for an eye. Zep'll see to that."

Zep advanced on the doorway and Tito stepped on inside. Behind him he heard Crane growl furiously at Neville.

"Godalmighty, you hone it fine! I'm sendin' a couple of the boys after your brother. You an' him an' me are goin' to have us a little powwow afore the two of you get us kilt without any stakes a man can count even on the table yet!"

Some of Crane's men hurried off to catch up horses. Directly they led them back to resaddle at the enclosure at the *jacals*. Before they were finished there were exclamations of surprise in the yard and riders came in from the west. Zep remained all too visible just outside the doorway and Tito prudently stayed away from it.

There was a murmur of talk he could not make out except that he recognized Blair Stanton's voice. Then the footfalls of a group approached. Zep stepped aside to clear the entry. Exterior light was nearly gone and it was dark in the little cubicle. Tito recognized the figures in silhouette.

Blair Stanton was first. He towed behind him the dishevelled, cowering figure of Rosa Martinez. She looked at Blair with a deep, white-faced aversion and hung back as though in appeal to Neville, who followed. Ted Crane was last. The others hung about outside, waiting curiously and with anticipation.

Rosa did not seem to have been harmed beyond outrage to her dignity. Tito's first reaction was a wave of relief. His message had not gone through to the Corona after all. He was still on his own.

Blair spun the cringing girl forward to face Tito. She saw him for the first time in the shadows. She ran to him with a sob in her voice and flung herself into his arms.

"Tito—oh, Tito, thank God!" she gasped. "I've been so afraid!"

"Easy, now," he said, trying to give her a cue. "What are you doing here? What happened?"

"I—I lamed my horse in the mountains yesterday. Above timberline on the far side of El Cumbre. Almost to the top. But we couldn't get over before dark. The leg stiffened in the cold. This morning she could hardly move, even on lead. I—I couldn't just leave him up there like that."

"Not you," Tito agreed gently. "Not that horse. Hell of a place to be set afoot."

"It was my fault. I should have led him across that slide. I knew it. But I was in such a hurry . . ."

She straightened in an apparent effort to get hold of herself.

"I knew Greta and Quelí were expecting me and that they'd be worried to death because I was late. I didn't get back down into timber on this side until way after noon and he was still limping too badly to ride. I should have headed to Mora. It was closer. But I thought I could make the Corona by supper."

Tito tightened his grip on her in reassurance. She was doing well.

"And my half brother met you," he prompted.

Rosa nodded tearfully. Tito knew she was in part putting on for the others, but there was an honest fear in her as well. He had no doubt it was justified. A Martinez of either sex was not easily demoralized.

"He recognized me from the office in Santa Fe. He thinks I was carrying a message for you. To your father."

"Me, entrust a woman with something I could do better?" Tito said. "He should know different if he's the Stanton he claims. It's all right, now. Here . . ."

He kicked his saddle around on the floor and lowered her to it.

"I smell coffee," he said to Crane. "Fetch her some."

Crane spoke to one of the men outside. Word was passed. A steaming cup was handed in. Rosa took it and sipped gratefully.

"Goddamn little wildcat," Blair said with some admiration. "Couldn't get a thing out of her. Too many witnesses. Kind of cramped my style. You try—or talk for her. What was the message she was supposed to deliver to the old man?"

Tito didn't answer. His half brother rocked forward suggestively on the balls of his feet.

"Want me to get a couple strong-arms in here to hold you again while I knock it out of you? Little blood might improve her memory."

"She told you," Tito said quietly. "She doesn't know. Because there wasn't any."

"Like hell!" Blair snorted. "You saw her in Santa Fe. She told you what we were up to."

"She did," Tito agreed. "After I dropped by the *palacio* to deliver an invitation from my sister and Jaime Henry's girl. They're old friends. It's visiting weather this time of year. That's all. It went no further. No message. I handle my own chores."

"Bullshit! You sent a warning, at least. Or suggested some scheme."

"Damn it, you wear on a man," Tito snapped irritably. "There isn't a kid on our grass that'd have the gall to run howling to Spence for help just because he flushed himself out a nest of snakes or a pack of mangy coyotes. Least of all me. He'd have beat my butt off for it before I was ten years old."

He turned to the girl.

"You'll have to stay the night, way it is. We'll see to your horse in the morning and get you on your way before Greta and Quelí start turning the hills upside down looking for you."

"Now you know we can't do that, brother," Blair said easily. "Let a pretty thing like this go riding off on her own to shoot off her mouth about what she's seen and heard?"

He stopped and chuckled.

"Funny how things work out. We keep her around, maybe she'll toll us in a couple more little ladies to keep us company and use for hostages—if you both aren't lying about your sister and her friend maybe looking for her. I left three of Crane's boys out on the Corona-Mora trail, just in case."

Tito saw Crane's eyes brighten at this. However, Neville Stanton protested sharply.

"Hold on! That's no part of the plan, Blair. Using girls hardly more than kids."

"You tell me," Blair said. "They'll be harder used before they're full grown." He reached down, caught Rosa's wrist, and pulled her up, spilling her coffee. "On your feet, honey. Finders keepers in this camp. I get lonesome and I feel a long night coming on."

Rosa shrank back and tried to free herself. Tito moved to intervene. He ran into the muzzle of Crane's gun.

"Leave be!" the ex-soldier warned sibilantly. "The man's boss."

Neville Stanton stepped quickly forward, his jaw set and the veins at his temples cording angrily.

"The hell he is!" he snapped.

His good hand dropped to his brother's wrist, pinioning it and breaking Blair's grip on the girl. At the same time his hook slashed horizontally like a scythe. Its point snagged both points of Blair's collar, barely missing flesh. Neville twisted the hook viciously, drawing up the collarband of the shirt until his brother's breath began to whistle in his constricted throat.

"Lay hand to her again and I'll rip you open from crotch to navel," Neville hissed. "Out—and take Crane with you!"

With a sudden, violent tug of reversal that rocked his brother, Neville freed the hook. He held it menacingly in the air before him, poised and ready. Tito saw livid fear of that pointed loop of steel in Blair's eyes as he staggered back, clawing open his twisted collar.

"All right," he gasped. "For chrissake, all right!"

But for all his fear, there was no forgiveness in his tone. He turned and reeled out of the *jacal*. Forgetting the drawn gun in his hand or unwilling to call attention to it, Crane backed hastily out after him. Neville faced Rosa Martinez.

"He mess with you?"

She hesitated, lowering her head.

"A little."

"There'll be no more of that. I promise."

Rosa lifted her face and instinctively reached for his hand in gratitude. When her fingers encountered the steel of the hook instead of flesh they closed up on it and she clasped her other hand firmly over the first.

"Mil gracias," she whispered. "Thank you—Neville."

Chapter 11

Twilight deepened. It became impossible to see across the *jacal*. Neville Stanton heard his half brother stir. A match rasped alight and was touched to the wick of a tin candle-lantern Tito had fished from his gear.

The girl from Santa Fe remained on Tito's grounded saddle. Aware of Neville's regard, she smiled tentatively at him. He asked her name. She gave it shyly. Neither spoke again. Tito also remained silent.

The sound of voices and occasional movement came from beyond the doorway. Those outside were settling for the night. Tension built in Neville. Crane and Blair were out there. They would have their heads together. Neither was a patient man.

However, when an approach was made it was a peace offering. Three steaming tin plates, coffee, and a canteen of water were put down outside the door. Tito glanced at Neville in query. He nodded. Tito went to the door and returned with the food. They ate in continuing silence.

Neville marvelled at the girl. When they had finished she took the utensils unbidden to the door and stacked them there without a glance into the night beyond. Returning, she took the blanket Tito tossed her and curled up against his saddle. In a remarkably short time she was sound asleep.

Neville could not tell if her confidence was in him because of his gesture of defense against Blair or in the silent half brother impassively watching him across the flickering lantern. He surmised the latter and felt a vague tug of regret.

Too often a man could only measure himself by his reflection in the eyes of others. Usually those of a woman were the most revealing. It would please him to stand tall before this one.

He was physically startled when Tito spoke, indicating the sleeping girl.

"You meant what you promised her?" he asked softly. "They'll leave her be?"

"You'll see."

"No. I won't be here."

Neville watched this other half-shadow of himself, trying to read intent, but the face and eyes remained expressionless.

"No?" he asked. "Then why the hell did you come in the first place, alone? What did you mean to do when we showed up?"

"You and Blair?" Tito shrugged. "Kick some sense into you. Run you off. Plant you, if it came to that."

"Now?"

"Crane makes a difference. I doubt he listens any better than your brother. Too many graves for one man to dig—all at once. So it's something else. I'll trouble you for my gun."

"You've changed your mind, then. You'll talk to the old man—or bring him here so we can talk to him—alone?"

"No. You make a mistake. Spence isn't that old. I'll handle this on my own. The gun—"

Neville drew Tito's gun from his belt. It was a Navy Colt, which had become familiar enough during and since the war. But it had been beautifully reworked by a master smith. The barrel had been shortened and lightened. The grips had been finely shaved down. It seemed more a boy's weapon than a man's, but it had a nice feeling of balance in his hand. He knew it was a special weapon with special significance to its owner. He shook his head and shoved the gun back under his belt. A sweep of his hook indicated the sleeping girl.

"You're staying till we've made our deal. We can

hold an army off here and you're too valuable to us, same as she is. Blair's right about that. I don't like it, but we've got to use what we can. If what you told us about her's true—a friend of your sister and all—the old man'll sweat some over us having her. And you. When he's sweat enough he'll come around. Even Spencer Stanton."

Tito drew a deep breath of resignation. It almost sounded like a sigh of regret. One of his crossed legs straightened with the snap of a sprung steel trap. The toe of his boot caught the candle-lantern squarely, driving it straight into Neville's face.

The ball of flame at the wick seemed to explode as it shot toward him, implanting its expanding brilliance on the retinal nerves of his eyes. He felt the bite of hot tin and molten wax as the lantern struck the bridge of his nose and clattered softly away.

Neville realized the light must have been extinguished upon impact and the *jacal* plunged into total darkness but the retinal image of the flaming wick remained, momentarily blinding him as effectively as the sear of a white-hot poker. He rolled away, giving ground to get at his own gun, but Tito's body crashed into him only an instant behind the lantern.

His hand was torn away from his holster and the gun it contained. His wrist was ground into the coarse cinder ash of the floor by a pinioning knee. Tito's other knee rammed in under the vee of his ribs, driving the air so completely from his lungs that he lacked wind for oath or outcry.

His hook, usually so effective at close quarters, was seized by the laced leather gauntlet that bound it to the stump of his wrist and was twisted so mercilessly that the elbow above was wracked almost beyond endurance. A thumb scraped up under his ear, forcing his head back and bearing down mercilessly on some artery or nerve there. Neville felt consciousness waver and Tito's gun was tugged out from under his belt.

Suddenly, seemingly between one instant and the

next, the weight of the hard, pinioning body above him was gone and he was lying limply on the *jacal* floor. Clumsily, like in a childhood dream when frantic attempts at movement had the frustrating speed of cold-poured molasses, he rolled over and got his knees under him.

He found his half-spilled gun and lumbered unsteadily to his feet, gasping for air and chafing at the numbed bruised spot beneath his ear. Shaking his head and blinking away the remnant retinal image of candle-flame lingering before his eyes, he lunged for the silhouetted starshine of the doorway.

Before he could reach the opening another driving body struck him at the ankles in the darkness, cutting him down again. He fell heavily across Rosa Martinez. She gasped with hurt at the impact but clutched him fiercely to her, body writhing to entangle him.

"Keep down!" she hissed in his ear. "For the love of God don't make him shoot!"

Half dazed and not fully comprehending, Neville obeyed. After a few panting breaths the girl beneath him released her grip and untwined her hampering legs.

"He's gone, now," she gasped. "I owed you that."

Astonished, Neville realized she meant what she said. She believed she had saved his life. Softly running footsteps approached outside. Blair's voice came, guarded and urgent.

"Neville, get out here!"

"Go ahead," Rosa whispered. "You'll see."

Neville heaved up and stumbled out into the faint starshine. Blair was there with one of Crane's men.

"Watch them," Blair ordered the Johnny Blue, indicating the door of the *jacal*. "Don't let them even show their faces till we knew what's up." He seized Neville's arm. "Come on. Quiet, for chrissake."

He moved swiftly away. Neville followed as silently as he could. Crane and the men who remained with him were bunched against the lava wall surrounding the *ja-*

cals. Some saddles and gear were stacked nearby. The silent group turned toward Neville and Blair as they hurried up. The movement revealed a limp form draped over the rough stones of the wall, face to the sky.

"Bastards sneaked up and got him," Crane whispered. "Just now, I think. Body's still warm. God knows how many of 'em out there."

"See anybody—hear anything?" Neville asked.

"Slim's been on sentry since dark," Blair answered. "Not a sound. Got his rifle and powder."

"A saddle and some gear gone, too," Crane added. "Damn that lyin' half brother of yours, claimin' he was alone and no tip-off sent the ranch. We wouldn't even of knowed till time to relieve Slim if I hadn't gone yonder to pee and seen him lyin' here. Poor devil. No tellin' when they'll jump another of us. Or rush the lot at once."

"The hell there isn't!" Blair growled. "Fetch Tito out here and we'll damn soon find out."

"Wait," Neville said.

He picked up the sentry's limp wrist. There was a pulse, slow but steady.

"He's not dead. Come around directly. Somebody scratch me a light."

"And give some night-shooting son of a bitch a mark?" Crane protested angrily. "No wonder you Rebs lost the war, the damn-fool orders you give!"

"I give them, just the same," Neville answered firmly. "Scratch me a light."

There was a moment of motionless indecision. It was Blair who finally complied, nervously cupping the flame of the match from the outer night. Neville caught the unconscious sentry's hair and turned his head, pulling it far back to expose his throat. The white-rimmed red mark of an efficiently impressed thumb-bruise lay just below the upturned ear. He let the head roll slackly back.

"Only one man out there," he said. "High-tailing it

out of here as fast as he can go. For his horse, likely.
With a borrowed rifle and saddle. To hell and gone by
daylight."

"What makes you so damned sure?" Crane demanded.

"Tito. He gave me the same medicine."

"Christalmighty! The girl gone, too?"

"She's still in the shanty. He left her."

"Why the hell'd he do that? It don't make sense."

"He didn't say."

"Stow the smart answers, Stanton!" Crane snapped.
"You've diddled this up enough already. If word didn't
get to your old man before it's sure on its way now."

"I don't think so."

"Think?" Crane exploded. "You? With what? They'll
be at us like a wolf pack. I ain't sitting here waiting for
'em. Not till we got a bygod sight more to dicker with
'em over than a couple scraps of paper an' a maybe
legal right that won't be worth a hoot in hell if powder
starts to burn. We got to hurt 'em and hurt 'em good
whiles we got the chance."

He swung on his companions.

"Over the wall," he ordered. "Catch up every horse
you can lay hand to. Tito Stanton ain't the only one that
can ride in the dark. We're goin' huntin', and not for
table-meat."

Neville clicked the claw on his hook in exasperation
and angrily started to protest the folly of attempting anything until there was light and they had a clearer indication of what Tito himself intended to do. Only then
could they plan properly and at minimum risk. This was
no small-stakes game to be played in high-handed, spur-
of-the-moment roughneck fashion.

Blair gripped his arm sharply, silencing him.

"Let be," he whispered urgently. "His back's up and
we've got to have him. Give him his head till he cools a
bit. I'll handle him. When money talks he listens fast."

"Money?"

Blair reached into his shirt and slid a worn pouch

partially into view. Neville heard the clink of minted metal. He recognized its source at once.

"You did knock him off that bridge in the pass!" he charged accusingly.

"When opportunity knocks . . . Thought it might come in handy before we could lay hands on some of our own."

"Where the hell was it when they searched us?"

"I was burying it when they came up. No man'll dig under another's dunghill. All I had to do was kick it out when I went back to finish my job. Little payment in earnest now, he'll get reasonable quick. And stay that way."

"You damned fool!" Neville said furiously. "Show Crane that and he'll kill you in your tracks."

"Might want to, but he won't. No proof. Gold all looks the same."

"Oh, Christ, it's not that, you knothead. He knows we didn't have it a few hours ago. Either one of us. He took pains enough to make sure. So it was hidden. Had to be a reason for that. He won't need any more proof. Get rid of it, right now. Someplace he won't find it. If he does, we're dead. Both of us. And don't keep any more goddamned secrets from me."

"Look," Blair said harshly, his earlier anger flooding back. "I'm with Crane. You've balled this up aplenty with your blasted pussyfooting. Any more orders, you keep them to yourself!"

Blair stormed off into the darkness after the others.

Chapter 12

A faint night wind came down from the mountains across the *malpaís* as the badlands lost the accumulated heat of the day. Tito moved with this breath of air at his back, deliberately letting it carry his scent before him.

Domesticated working horses did not have the incredibly keen senses of their free-running, untamed kin. However, enough of the wild remained in them—at least on the high grass—to put the shrewdest human stalker to shame. A dismounted man could save himself a long night search by letting nature work for him.

He found his mount not far from where it had disappeared when he turned it loose on arrival. Rather, the animal found him. It ambled in toward the body-smell of its master, whinnying softly for familiar companionship. Tito answered almost inaudibly. The horse nuzzled to him in the darkness. He reassured it by touch and swung up the saddle he carried. The animal shied a little from the unfamiliar weight and contour of the old McClellan rig for which he had been forced to settle.

He had no liking for these butt-busting issue hulls and regretted that he had not been able to bring his own, but the risk in getting out and over the wall surrounding the *jacals* so encumbered had seemed too great. It was a small inconvenience. Horse and rider could put up with it for a few hours. With luck they would have a short ride.

With his mount saddled and bridled, Tito adjusted the stirrup leathers for a quick mount if necessary. Thrusting his borrowed rifle into the service boot laced to the McClellan, he led off afoot. Even the best saddle pony was poor at picking sound footing in the dark. He kept to grass where he could and worked westward toward fairer country and the Corona-Mora road.

Blair had said he had left three men there when he brought Rosa Martinez into the camp. The first order of business was to dispose of them according to the stand they took. It had to be done before they halted one of the *vaqueros* or some other chance traveller, and before Spence Stanton learned of the invaders in the heart of his empire.

Haste would not be necessary. There would be no night traffic between the two sections of the ranch. Knowing he would have to bypass the camp at Ojos Negros, he stopped frequently to listen, but his horse sensed nearby movement before he did.

He felt the ripple of hide over taut shoulder muscles as the animal's head came up and he froze in his tracks. Men afoot were casting about in the darkness, searching for their own freed mounts. He thought two were very close and others prowling a little farther off. His escape had been discovered.

The searchers sensibly made no unnecessary sounds, but they had no understanding of how even breathing carried at night in these mountains. Tito dropped his rein-ends to the ground, knowing his horse would stand as though anchored, and backed away a few paces. He wanted no confrontation so close to the *jacals,* if he could avoid it.

His horse, deprived of the reassurance of his immediate presence, snorted softly.

"Here's one of the spooky bastards," a muted voice called in exasperated relief, even closer than he expected. "Try to work in on the offside to keep him turned toward me."

"I think there's another one over in here someplace, too," another voice replied.

"Yeah, well, let be a minute. I'm almost onto this one."

Tito caught the faint loom of a cautiously approaching silhouette. The man was carrying a halter in one hand and his belt-gun in the other. The precaution was a measure of his wariness but it made catching up with a horse in the dark no easier. The Johnny Blue saw Tito's horse but apparently not the saddle on its back for he stepped eagerly forward, the halter raised and ready.

"Easy, now, boy," he coaxed softly.

The horse danced nervously around in pirouette but did not drag the grounded reins. Tito could now hear the second man's approach. His jaw clamped grimly. The odds were getting a little sticky if silence was to be preserved. He did not like the necessity but slid his own gun from its holster. The chop of a pistol barrel could not be measured as precisely as that of a mauled fist and he was still reluctant to draw first blood.

The thought was a nicety under the circumstances, he knew, but his father had warned him against violence with his half brothers and Spencer Stanton made the rules on the Corona. He always had and he inbred them deeply. All others obeyed them if they could. Or they answered for it.

They had long called Spence the toughest man in the Territory. That he was, with Jaime Henry and Abelardo at Mora close seconds. But every man had his fair chance with any of them unless he cut the odds too short. That was the way it was. It always had been.

Half a dozen paces from Tito the approaching man stiffened, staring at the horse.

"Christ, this one's saddled," he called sharply, letting his voice rise. "Watch yourself, Ben!"

He dropped the halter and spun about, his gun sweeping with him as his eyes searched the night beyond the horse. His hand forced, Tito leaped forward. The man heard him and centered his gun, sighting by ear before he could separate his target from the darkness.

Tito struck swiftly in midstride. He felt the sickening give of crushed bone. The Johnny Blue's gun did not fire and he dropped soundlessly in his tracks.

Tito vaulted over his body as it fell, now guiding himself by sound alone. He heard the catch of the second man's breath at the sudden eruption of movement and veered toward it. The uneasy horse snorted again, drawing the forewarned man's attention for a precious instant. Tito plowed into him at full speed. They went down together in a grunting thrash of arms and legs.

This one, too, had his belt-gun clear. Tito got his hand onto the weapon and took the smash of the hammer on his grasping thumb as the trigger was pulled. In too cramped and awkward a position to swing, Tito rammed the muzzle of his own weapon clumsily forward into the man's face. He heard teeth break and a choking outcry.

His opponent writhed desperately, trying to tear his gun from Tito's pained and precarious grip. Still wedging the hammer of the weapon back from caps and charge, Tito got his knees under him and brought the barrel of his own gun down hard.

The threshing beneath him ceased with a shudder. He came unsteadily to his feet and listened intently. The only sound was his own labored breathing and the roar of blood in his ears.

Freeing his aching thumb from beneath the hammer of the Johnny Blue's gun, he thrust the weapon in his belt and returned to his horse. The smell of blood was there in the night now. The frightened animal danced away with flattened ears but training held. The grounded reins did not drag. Tito caught them up and led off again.

In a few rods the trailing animal quieted. Presently Tito breathed easier, knowing he had by now worked past the camp at the *jacals*. Any other horse hunters Crane and his half brothers had sent out were obviously further back into the lava toward the lesser springs there. Whatever their intent, he had a sufficient lead.

Half a mile further on he stumbled onto the abandoned track that had reached in from the old Corona-Mora stage road when there had been a rest stop at

Ojos Negros. He swung to saddle and let his horse pick its own pace on this better footing.

The sentries Blair had left posted when he brought Rosa Martinez into the lava camp had chosen to make camp for their own comfort rather than for the efficiency of the watch they were supposed to keep. Tito found their bivouac by the acrid scent of recently quenched wood-ash in the night air.

It lay hard by the old stage road, but in a hollow where a small tributary of the Cimarroncito emerged from the mountains. It was sheltered by the first of the pines that clothed the slopes above it. The stream was a three-foot rivulet at this season, but the water was sweet and cold and there was patchy meadow grass for their horses.

North and south the road rose to higher ground, exposing their position to view and approach from either direction. It was not a hunter's camp or one of seasoned high-country travellers, but it was protected from the wind, snug and comfortable under the circumstances. They had eaten long ago, snuffed their fire, and now slept.

Tito crossed the road beyond earshot on the south slope and worked into the timber before turning back. Reaching the little creek upstream of the sleeping men, he dismounted and left his horse. The sound of even so insignificant a flow was an effective way to drown out the noise of a stealthy approach.

He worked down the creek-bank as silently as he could. He knew that even outlander Johnny Blues would know enough to hobble their horses below them to protect their own water, so he had little fear of spooking the animals. His only concern was that he not step on one of the sleepers before he could precisely locate them.

The caustic smell of wet wood-ash grew stronger. He caught a whiff of the acrid, curiously pleasant scent of sweated blankets and saddle leather, and knew he was almost upon them. Dropping to all fours to lower his silhouette, he crept forward. His hand touched the heavy bullhide leather of a pair of saddlebags on the ground. His reaching fingers encountered the steel of a rifle barrel slanted across them to keep the lock from the ground.

He silently pulled back the hammer and drew the percussion cap from the priming nipple of the weapon. Letting the hammer gently back down to half-cock, he stretched flat, head close to the ground. In this position he could make out other silhouettes.

There was another pair of heavy saddlebags nearby and the worn canvas cylinder of an issue duffel bag—the kind that had been most troopers' home away from home during the war. It was a singularly impractical way to carry necessaries since it opened at only one end and had to be completely emptied to sort immediate needs from its contents.

Beyond were the three saddles, serving as headrests for the blanket-wrapped sleepers. Tito was amused that they were laid out parallel in a neat row with military precision. Once a soldier always a soldier. In this country a man learned soon enough to stretch his bed where the ground was softest and most level, whichever way. It saved a lot of aching backs.

Presently he located the other two rifles leaned against a sapling, shot, powder, and cap pouches dangling from belt or shoulder straps from their forepieces. He wriggled carefully to them and disarmed them as he had the first. Only then did he turn his attention in earnest to the sleepers.

The gunbelt of the first was twisted about the low pommel of the saddle against which he rested so that the weapon was at hand. Reaching over the sleeper, Tito eased the belt-gun from its holster. Unwilling to risk the sound of the cylinder ratchet, which might ensue as he rotated it to remove the caps from the priming nipples to disarm the rifles, he carried the gun with him as he wriggled on to the next man.

He found belt and holster rolled up on the ground beside the saddle, but the weapon itself was missing. Swearing softly, Tito tried with infinite care to turn back a corner of the sleeper's blanket, but it was pulled tightly over the man's shoulder and pinned beneath him. Yet the gun had to be there

It was a widely accepted belief that a percussion piece would not fire dependably unless it was kept in some proximity to a man's body heat. Some notion the fulminate in the cap functioned erratically when chilled by night air. Tito had known many otherwise practical and experienced men who habitually slept with this uncomfortable bedfellow beneath the blankets for this reason.

Tito occasionally did so himself, but only when rain, snow, or heavy dew might harm the piece or damp out the priming hole between nipple and chamber. Scrabbling around in the folds of bed or blanket for his weapon when it was needed in a hurry was not his idea of sensible preparedness under any other circumstance.

He tugged gently at the blanket again but it would not give. He broke off a slender tendril of grass. Usually a man, his clothing, and his blanket stank enough after a few days in the open to discourage the tiny winged and crawling creatures of the night, but occasionally they were voracious or determined enough to brave it. When they did, they searched out where the juices were—the ear, the corner of an eye, the mouth.

He brushed the stem of grass gently and slowly across the upturned side of the sleeper's face, a minuscule nocturnal visitor unhurriedly searching. There was no response at first. He tried again. A muscle twitched. The third time the uppermost shoulder heaved up, pulling the blanket loose to free an arm, and the man's hand scrubbed across his cheek to brush away the intruder.

As the arm freed, lifting the blanket, Tito reached swiftly beneath it. The gun was there, almost in the armpit of the undermost arm. It came away without

touching flesh. The man grunted softly, recovered himself, and sank again into heavy breathing. Tito moved
on to the third sleeper. His belt-gun lay in its holster
beneath his hat on a neatly folded saddlecloth within
reach.

Tito secured it and wormed to the creek. He slid the
three weapons into the water, tucking them into a little
undercut of the bank where they would not readily be
seen. It really made little difference. In a few moments
they would be soaked enough that they would have to
be thoroughly dried, cleaned, recharged, and primed
before they could be fired again.

Well aware that they were three to his one, even
without their weapons, Tito knew that deeply sleeping
men were often completely unpredictable in their first
instant's response to sudden arousal by an unexpected
alarm. On the other hand, if they could instinctively
identify as normal the place and circumstance, it
seemed to reassure them and permit a normal awaken-
ing.

Fumbling a smooth stone the size of a biscuit from
the creek-bed, he flung it off in a high arc downstream
where the Johnny Blues' hobbled horses were. It
glanced off a tree and dropped. There was instant com-
motion among the horses. The sleeping men sat up in
unison as though pulled by the same string.

Tito gave them a moment to realize their belt-guns
were missing, then spoke quietly.

"Tito Stanton here. Stay in your blankets. Right
where you are."

The two nearest obeyed, their eyes searching anxiously for him. The one closest to the rifles leaning
against the tree did not. Tito heard the rustle of his
movement as he quit his blanket and the slap of his
hand against one of the weapons, batting the ammunition pouches dangling from its forestock free.

The hammer of the weapon clicked swiftly back to
cock and dry-fired against the disarmed priming nipple.
Thinking it was merely a not infrequent misfire, the

Johnny Blue recocked and tried again before realizing the primer had been removed and there was no time to replace the missing cap.

Tito rose to his feet and stepped forward so all three could see his moving silhouette in the darkness as he approached.

"Savvy, now?" he asked the man with a rifle. "Since you're up, make a light."

The man discarded his useless weapon and knelt by a pair of saddlebags, rummaging within. Alert to the possibility of a spare handgun there, Tito watched closely. However, the searching hand produced only a candlestub and a match rasped alight.

The candle threw long, distorted shadows across the makeshift camp. Tito's was the longest of all, an effect he had intended. He drew his belt-gun and rocked it tentatively in his hand.

He let the message soak in for a long, silent moment, then reholstered the weapon.

"Bring in your horses," he ordered. "You're breaking camp."

The two still in their blankets hastily kicked free. All three drew on their boots. Scrambling for bridles, they stumbled off down the creek, looking uneasily back over their shoulders. When they disappeared, Tito dumped the issue duffel bag he had earlier noticed on a blanket. He collected the shot-pouches, powder flasks, and cap-boxes that had been with the rifles and dumped them into the bottom of this.

When the three returned with their horses, he had finished repacking the contents of the bag in on top of the ammunition and relacing the open end.

"Get your gear up and wipe out any sign of this camp," he said. "You won't be using it again."

The Johnny Blues did not protest or question but fell hurriedly to. It was clumsy work by the scant light of the single candle flickering on a deadfall, but Tito stood inflexibly by and it was quickly done. He gestured for them to mount.

"Think you can find your way back to those *jacals* in the lava?" he asked.

They were doubtful.

"When it's this dark?" one answered. "Maybe. Reckon we can try."

"Don't," Tito warned sharply, "if you want to stay alive. Follow down this creek. It'll bring you to the Cimarroncito directly. Keep to the near bank. It's mostly grass and easy going. Stay east along the Cimarroncito till it swings north. That'll get you past the *malpaís* and you'll have water.

"Have the sun by then, too. When you quit the Cimarroncito, hold straight on east till you hit the Trail. Maybe forty miles. You've been on it before. You're on your own there. Santa Fe or whichever way suits you. But damn you, don't turn back. Don't even look back. If you're ever caught on Stanton land again you'll be shot on sight. *Entienden?*"

They looked uncertainly at each other.

"What about the rest—Ted Crane—your brothers?"

"That's their problem. You've got yours. Don't borrow more. Come daylight you'll find your powder in the bottom of that duffel bag and you've got your rifles. Now get the hell out of here!"

They kicked up their horses and rode off downstream. When the sounds of their departure faded, Tito picked up the candle and went over the campsite, scuffing out any obvious signs of their presence that the Johnny Blues had missed. It was not skillfully enough done to fool an Indian or any other conscientious searcher, but he thought no casual passerby would be likely to note evidence of trespass and the first of the usual afternoon thunderstorms would complete the task.

He snuffed the candle and headed upstream toward his own horse.

Chapter 13

Two of Crane's men did not reappear from the stygian darkness of the scattered grass pockets in the *malpaís* about Ojos Negros. Others found their horses and brought them in but reported no trace of the missing Johnny Blues. They had not responded to the hails to which their anxious companions finally resorted.

There was much alarmed and uneasy speculation at the wall about the *jacals* over their absence as the rest saddled up at Crane's orders. Neville was restless with his own apprehensions. Rosa Martinez had curled up with the blanket against the saddle Tito had left behind and was apparently sleeping soundly again. Neville slipped quietly from the *jacal*.

At careless expenditure of the scant fuel available in this barren place, a fire had been built against the surrounding wall to serve as a beacon for those searching the night for their horses. The flames still gave enough light to aid in saddling. Every man in the camp was there with the horses, getting gear up.

They eyed Neville with hostile wariness as he approached. Blair and Ted Crane were still angry. Their mistrust and disapproval had communicated to the others. Blair spoke over his shoulder as Neville came up.

"Look," he warned truculently, jerking his cinch up tight. "No more goddamned argument!"

Neville knew some sort of accommodation would have to be reached with his brother and Crane. A measure of conciliation would be forced upon him by the circumstances. But he could not risk losing any more of his shrinking authority if he could avoid it.

"Only one thing worse than one damned fool with his back up," he said uncompromisingly. "That's two of you. Like it or not, we're in this together. For chrissakes, simmer down and listen to reason—"

He was interrupted by a hoarse cry from a man on the far side of Blair's horse. Rigid, his face blanched, the Johnny Blue was staring into the night.

The ghastly figure of a man was reeling out of the darkness toward the fire. He was barely able to keep his feet. His arms hung slackly. He staggered spraddle-legged from side to side as he came. His boots were rocking and buckling at the ankles. He was almost upon them before Neville recognized him as one called Ben, one of the pair who had not returned from chasing the horses.

His lips were pulped and swollen grotesquely open. Half a dozen of his front teeth were missing, leaving his mouth a gory hole in his face. His scalp was deeply split and an ugly blue welt, the size and length of a pistol barrel, protruded from above one eyebrow far back toward the crown of his hatless head.

The wound had bled with the curious profuseness of such head injuries and he was wheezing hoarsely at the effort the stumbling movement cost him. Two of his fellows belatedly leaped forward in time to catch him as he started to fall. They dragged him to the fire. Another flung down a saddlepad to keep his head from the grit underfoot. Crane knelt for a quick look and barked an order.

"Fetch a nose-bucket of water."

A man sprinted off toward the spring and loped back with a dripping canvas bag. Crane callously upended it over the battered face and head. The injured man gasped spasmodically at the additional shock.

"What happened?" Crane demanded.

The man's eyes rolled but speech would not form in the shattered mouth. Crane shook him insistently.

"Goddamn it, what happened?"

The man choked and clumsily spat out a great gout

of coagulated blood. The effort was herculean but
words came.

"Levi, too," he mumbled thickly. "He's out there.
Dead, I think."

The eyes closed in a spasm of pain.

"Who was it?" Crane demanded again. "How many?
How long ago?"

"Don't know. Never even saw 'em. Onto me that
quick. Levi—"

The man coughed again. Fresh blood came from his
nose. He struggled a moment. Then the contorted features slackened. The eyes did not reopen. Crane surged
to his feet, snatched up the uncharred end of a stick of
sun-bleached wood from the fire, and swung it about
his head to fan brighter flame at the burning end.

"Come on, some of you," he yelled. "Fan out. He
can't a come far."

He plunged off into the darkness. Others seized similar makeshift torches and ran after him, swiftly becoming receding blobs of light.

Blair stood looking down at the injured man with a
savage expression of accusation, as though the bloody
figure on the ground had somehow done him grave personal harm. Neville bent and reached for one of the
limp wrists. Blair's look shifted to him.

There was fear behind the question in Blair's eyes.
Neville suddenly realized there was fear behind the sav-
agery surfacing in him as well. Not fear of the concrete
and the rational—the known and anticipated. Blair
could cope with those. Neville had seen him do so often
enough when the chips were down. No great heroics,
except for show when the risk was small. That was not
Blair's style. But he was competent in a tight spot.

He did not fear the enemy—the Corona and the New
Mexico Stantons. They were men. Neville thought it
was the shadow they cast upon their land. Maybe the
land itself. The unknown and the unknowable. The unexpected and the unimaginable were getting to him. Si-

lent death in the night. For that Neville felt sympathy. He was shaken himself.

He rose slowly from the body of the dead man, shaking his head. Something snapped in Blair. His lips skinned back from his teeth.

"You stupid, stubborn ass!" he said thinly. "So you'd try to bargain with the old man!"

Neville didn't realize what was coming until his brother's fist caught him flush on the jaw, knocking him under the hoofs of the nearest horses. Wild and unreasoning fury was up in his attacker, uncontrolled. Before Neville could recover, Blair was at him, blindly shouldering the horses aside and jerking him to his feet.

"We'll settle this right now!" he raged. "You got us into it but by god I'll get us out, full pockets to boot, if we have to kill the whole bastard greaser line. From here on I'm giving the orders and you'll damned well take 'em!"

He swung again before Neville could regain balance or even get a guard up. He was hit, knocked down, kicked, yanked to his feet again so swiftly he could not overcome his initial astonishment. The slugging blows came in a hail against which there was no defense.

Then others were intervening, piling on Blair from behind, hauling him back, separating them and pointing into the night. Blobs of torchlight were growing larger as Crane and the other searchers returned.

They came up to the fire, bringing the body of the second missing man with them. They dumped it in the cinders beside that of the first. Neville saw that the Johnny Blue's whole foreskull had been caved in above the bridge of his nose. He, too, had not known what hit him.

Blair was chafing at bruised knuckles, his eyes still dark with storm. Neville dabbed at the corner of his mouth. A little blood came away on his fingers. Crane looked at them both.

"Now what the hell?" he asked sourly.

"Settling something," Blair answered. "I'm taking over."

"Time," Crane grunted. "It'd been me or you, directly. May be, anyway, afore we're done."

He looked at the men crowding in.

"Two down on us, first time around. Damned if we're going to be nibbled off like corn on a cob." His eyes challenged Blair. "Call it or get off the pot, damn it."

"We'll ride," Blair said harshly. "I left three more staked on the Corona-Mora road. We'll pick them up and see if we can even the score, stack it some our way if we can. Soon's it's light enough to hunt. Hit fast the first chance we get and duck back in here before we can get cut off."

"Then what?"

"Wait it out and do it again as soon as we can. The old man or Tito or any of the rest won't take that too long. And if they trespass we got 'em by the short hair with it all going our way."

Crane nodded approval.

"Now you're talking. With a bonus for that heavy-handed, fast-gun half brother of yours. I think Hook, here, is right. It was just him out there tonight. He got Ben and Levi like he damned near did Slim. Trespassin', too. So the blood's on him. Cut him down and we've blowed Old Man Stanton and his whole blasted crew clean out of the saddle with one shot."

"I'll pay that bonus myself," Blair said. "On the spot. Five gold double-eagles, cash on the barrel-head, to the man who takes him."

Crane nodded at Neville.

"What about him? He's made it plain this ain't exactly to his taste. And that girl you brung in——"

"We may need her later. One way or another. They'll stay. Where's to go from here afoot? Take his gun. And Tito's rifle from the shack."

Hands were laid hold of Neville and his gun yanked from his holster. Zep and another man hurried off with a torch toward the *jacal* where Rosa Martinez was sleeping. High, wild recklessness was building in Blair as his confidence in command grew. Neville knew further protest was useless while he was in the grip of such an ungoverned mood, and he remained silent.

Zep and his companion returned with Tito's gun.

"Still sleeping," Zep reported in answer to Blair's questioning look about the girl.

Smiling with satisfaction, Blair stepped up to Neville. He braced himself instinctively, unsure of his brother's intent, but hands seized him again.

"One more thing," Blair said. He took a clasp knife from his pocket and snapped it open. "Just to make sure. You've always held I'm not half the man you are. Well—"

Seizing Neville's hook suddenly, he slid the blade of the knife under the lacings of the gauntlet that secured it to the stump of the severed wrist and slashed them through.

"Now you're not half the man I am."

Jerking the hook free and waving it mockingly as he moved, Blair wheeled to his horse and swung up.

"Let's ride!" he yelled.

He touched spurs and headed into the night. The Johnny Blues scrambled up and followed. Crane was last. He checked near Neville as though for a final word, then thought better of it. Perhaps it had already been said.

Neville remained motionless until he, too, had vanished and the receding sound died. He did not know how long he had been staring morosely into the ebbing fire when a soft scuffing in the ash and cinder under foot drew his attention. He lifted his head.

Rosa Martinez was leaning against the lava wall a yard away.

"You weren't sleeping after all."

"No," she agreed. "Only pretending. It seemed wisest, the mood they were in."

He nodded.

"Yes."

"Did they all go—no guard or sentries?"

"What for? No guns or horses, either," Neville answered flatly, chafing the stump of his wrist.

Rosa looked at the two dead men beyond the fire.

"See why I had to keep you from trying to follow Tito?" she asked. "The Stantons are like that. They do what has to be done. Their way. Alone if they can. Something about it's too big a ranch to double up on jobs when one man's enough."

"Big men," Neville said wryly.

"Yes," the girl agreed simply. "Big enough. I said the Stantons were like that."

She paused a moment, looking up at him.

"All of them."

Neville shook his head and absently chafed his maimed wrist again.

"I take that back," Rosa said. "One of them isn't! He did that on purpose—deliberately—uh—disarmed you, handicapped you. So you couldn't do anything."

"Hell, I'm not all that helpless!" Neville snapped. "But something's come over him. He'd never have even tried it before."

"I'm not sure. He was thinking a long way ahead. Even back in Santa Fe. You're supposed to be partners, aren't you?"

"Since the war, anyway."

"Did you ever look at that deed he had me make out for those scrip warrants he brought in—closely, I mean?"

"No," Neville said. "Only the map with it, trying to find our way in."

"Then look, now."

"Can't. He still has it on him."

"He had me draw it to Blair Stanton. Only to him, Neville. That was the way the warrants were drawn. Naturally I thought—"

"Naturally," Neville agreed.

Ice froze in his veins. The cold tide of an anger he

had never known before. The heat could come later.
The fury and the showdown. It was enough now to
know that what had been planned as a gentleman's
game, an audacious gamble to be determined by reasonable means, had become something else. Perhaps it had
been from the beginning. And his brother had become
the enemy in a faithless instant.

"I think he meant what he said when he told you he
was taking over, Neville," Rosa continued. "I don't
think he intends you to have any part of whatever he
can get from Tito and his father. I think he believes he
can get more than you ever could or would and he's
gambling on that. We've got to get out of here. We've
got to find Tito before something terrible happens."

"No," Neville said stonily. "This is between Blair and
me, now. The hell with Tito and Spencer Stanton. The
hell with anything else. But first we've got to get you to
the Corona before Blair can lay hands on you again
with time to do something about it. Come on, move!"

He thrust her roughly back toward the *jacal*.

Chapter 14

They had a canteen of water, the boots on their feet, and Neville's belt with its empty holster. This against the *malpaís*. Some stubborn perversity made Neville retain his powder, shot, and caps even though he was weaponless. Rosa rolled the blanket Tito had left in the *jacal* and slung it over her shoulder.

"Don't weight yourself down," he protested. "There'll be no sleep till you're safe on the Corona."

"The sun," she said. "In this thin air. That's why the blanket Indians carry them. My people, too. Insulation when the sun's high. We may need it. Headquarters are a long way afoot."

They left the fire to burn itself out. For a long time it was a dull red eye behind them in the darkness, watching over the cinders where two dead men lay.

Rosa remembered the course of the wagon-track shunt by which Blair had brought her into Ojos Negros. After a while she contrived to find it, more by luck than skill. They welcomed its smoother going and the saving on their footgear and plodded westward toward the undefined black wall, the mountains, against stars.

In about an hour a subtle change began. Very slowly a curious, purplish aura began to glow about the topmost peaks, etching only the very summits in silhouette. The source of the shimmering light seemed behind the mountains, beyond them, as though the sun were threatening to reverse itself and rise above the wrong horizon.

As the deep, impenetrable blue-black of the night washed more and more rapidly away, the strength and

color of the alpenglow changed swiftly into a great sash
of flaming red. This touched the snowy summits of the
peaks afire and raced down their gaunt flanks at ever-
increasing speed. When it reached the base of the
mountains, the rim of the sun thrust its arc above the
gently curving horizon-line of the *malpaís* and the unbroken grassed flatlands beyond, far off to the east.

The two sources of light joined. Day had come.

Neville Stanton found that he had unconsciously
halted in his tracks to watch the incredible display.
Rosa Martinez was a pace or two ahead, smiling back
at him.

"Something like three hundred and fifty days a year,"
she said. "They all start the same way unless there's a
storm. My mother says that if you're up early enough to
see the dawn in this country it's hard to make a bad
beginning anytime."

"We've made better ones," he grunted. "Both of us.
Know where Blair left those men on sentry out here?"

"Not exactly. But I think I can find it, now that it's
light."

They came presently to the "Y" where the shunt to
Ojos Negros joined the abandoned stage road winding
along the timber fringe at the base of the mountains.
Rosa turned north on this and they followed it into a
little vale where a small creek tumbled out onto the
grass.

There was no trace of a camp that Neville could locate but ample sign of recent passage. No care had been
taken to conceal it. The hoofprints of many horses
turned from the road and followed the creek off into the
eastward grasslands.

"Blair and Crane," Neville said bleakly. "Not too
long ago. Dark slowed 'em that much. Picked up the
sentries along here somewhere. Full company, now."

"Will they head straight for the Corona?" Rosa asked
anxiously.

"Doubt it, swinging east the way they did. Too big a
chance of biting off more'n they could chew, I'd guess.

Rather pick off their game one at a time with the odds in their favor. Likely split up to cover more ground. We've got to watch out some don't spot us. God help anybody on the Corona this morning!"

"If we only had horses—"

"Yeah—or wings. Come on. The sooner I can turn you over to somebody on the Corona the better."

Tito Stanton reapproached the *jacals* at Ojos Negros in the half-light of dawn. He saw at once that they were deserted and that no sentries remained. He was immediately alarmed for the safety of Rosa Martinez. Self-accusation stung him. He had thought Neville's presence would be a sufficient guarantee of her well-being. He had overestimated his older half brother's basic decency.

The *jacal* in which he and the girl had been held prisoner was empty. His rifle and blanket were gone but his saddle was still there. He swiftly exchanged it for the McClellan he had used for his escape. There was a scattering of gear in the compound where the Johnny Blues had bedded, so they obviously intended to return. He felt some relief at this.

Embers were still warm in the ashes of a fire against the outer wall of the compound. Two dead men lay sightless in the sun nearby. Tito could tell by their injuries that they were the two he had encountered in getting away. All signs were of hasty departure, but there was no evidence of the direction taken.

This did not trouble him. These were outlanders. Even Rosa Martinez did not know the *malpaís* well. The only route they could take, especially in the predawn darkness, would be toward the mountains to the Corona-Mora road, whatever their eventual purpose or destination. And he realized that because he had not expected them to make any move before daylight, he could have passed them on the way back in without being aware of it.

Now the burden was upon him. He had reduced their

numbers by five but they were still too many to capitulate and now that they were on the move with two of their number dead behind them, they were dangerous to anyone they encountered.

Swinging with relief into his own saddle, he turned again toward the mountains. Nearly back to the Corona-Mora road, a glint among the cinders some distance from the shunt caught his eye. A flash of sun on polished steel. He rode to it.

Lying in the pumice ash, nearly trodden under by those who had ridden over it, was Neville Stanton's hook and the thick leather gauntlet to which it was attached. The leather lacing that normally fastened it to its wearer's arm had been slashed through. Its owner had not parted with it willingly or by accident. And it had been callously discarded by whoever had taken it as though it were of no further use.

It could mean many things but one was plain. He had not misjudged his older half brother after all. Wherever the rest of the lot was taking Rosa Martinez, whatever their intentions as they rode, Neville was not party to it. If he was still with them he was not accompanying them of his own choice and volition.

Tito hurriedly remounted. He sunk the point of the hook firmly into the fork of his saddle where it could not become dislodged and lost again. Kicking up, he rode on urgently.

The cinders and ash of the *malpaís* would not hold imprints of passage clearly enough to be read. However, on the the creek above the Cimarroncito near where the sentries posted by Blair had been camped, the green sod was freshly trodden. The hoofprints turned off down the little stream and merged with the tracks of the three men Tito had disarmed and ordered out of Stanton country.

There was little doubt that the larger party would readily be able to trail the trio and swiftly overtake them. There was even less question that the three could

COMPAÑEROS 139

be easily persuaded to break out their unprimed rifles, recharge them, and rejoin their comrades.

Tito swore softly. His night foray into the sentries' camp had achieved no more than a temporary diversion at best. He had failed to achieve the further reduction in odds he had intended at no further loss of life. Time to forestall a full confrontation between the Corona crew and these now vengeful invaders was fast running out.

More than once, furtive intruders had been able to exist for weeks on the Corona, undetected and unsuspected. The vastness of the ranch made that possible with reasonable care at remaining hidden. But not when the aliens rode openly and as they pleased. Spencer Stanton swore that even the smoke of their fires had a different smell than those kindled by home hands.

A *paisano* family coming a great distance across the land to visit kith or kin at the ranch village or a *vaquero* at the lonely, endless task of riding for strays would spot them from a distant ridge and the word would go out. *Extranjeros!* From mouth to mouth the warning would travel swiftly. Strangers on the grass! The men of the Corona would gather then and ride.

If words would not suffice when the interlopers were found—and words were few with Spencer Stanton when others who had no business there were on his land—guns would speak. Guns emptied saddles, intruders and hands alike, friends—even family.

Tito started down the little creek, following the clotted tracks. In a few rods he pulled up sharply and swung down quickly for a closer look. In the still damp scuff of iron shoemarks and droppings were the prints of two pairs of boots. One pair was of Spanish last, slender and high-arched, with riding heels. Small boots, of the country.

The other pair of prints had been made by larger footgear, with broader heels and without the slight rounding of the soles to the welt of the uppers that betrayed any work from a New Mexican cobbler's bench.

The wearers, afoot, moving side by side, had crossed over the scuff of passage left by his half brothers and Ted Crane's hard-nosed, gold-seeking Johnny Blue drifters.

The two pairs of boots had forded the creek and struck straight north toward the distant headquarters of the Stanton ranch. Tito swung up, splashed across the creek, and spurred after them.

This stretch of the stage road between Rancho Mora and the Corona proper ran along the base of the foot-hills and out onto the treeless grass far enough to take advantage of flatter country and easier grades. Because of this Neville insisted on avoiding the track except where it occasionally ran through a down-reaching tongue of screening timber.

It made for harder going, costing them time and distance they could ill afford. But the higher elevations to which they generally kept gave them a broader view of the country ahead, and the cover on the slopes lessened the chance that a party of Crane's men with Blair or Crane or both might suddenly reappear from the east and catch them flat-footed in the open.

Neither Neville nor the girl spoke, conserving their breath by common assent and necessity. The sun was nearly two hours high when they saw the distant rider from a vantage. He was alone and driving a rogue steer ahead of him out of a small pocket of cutbank bad-lands.

"One of the *vaqueros* by the way he rides," Rosa Martinez said.

"Good. He can take you on in—if you think you'll be safe with him."

She smiled.

"Safer. He's armed."

"Let's get down where we can catch his eye."

They scrambled downslope toward an open patch of dun sidehill grass. When they emerged at a half run into this and pulled up in its midst in a position from which

they could signal with some hope of being seen, the rider below had disappeared momentarily behind a swell.

As they waited for the *vaquero* to reappear, other
horsemen streamed into view from the mouth of a shallow draw. They, too, were distant but close to the point
where the *vaquero* and the steer he was hazing had vanished. Neville recognized them at once and knowing
that he and the girl were in harsh silhouette where they
stood, he grabbed her with his good hand and pulled
her down onto the grass with him, hoping that they had
not been seen.

Apparently he had been in time. Blair and Crane and
their troop of renegade ex-soldiers spurred on like hunters running their quarry to earth. Neville and Rosa
watched helplessly as they disappeared where the *vaquero* and the steer had. There was no sound at this
distance. Only a thin, settling haze of dust left in the air.

Neville rose slowly, uncertainly, and lifted the girl.
Suddenly an almost simultaneous fusillade of four or
five shots rattled thinly in the morning air. Silence returned. Neville grabbed Rosa's hand and began running
across the open grass toward the nearest screen of timber. They crashed into this and through it to another
vantage a few rods farther on.

From this angle Blair, Crane, and their men reappeared in unhurried file, retracing their tracks. Suddenly
they pulled up, reacting to something above them,
closer at hand. They milled for a moment, then spurred
hastily into cover and waited there.

Neville searched the slopes above them and two more
riders came into view, working hurriedly down toward
them as though attracted by the sound of the shots.

"Women!" he grunted in astonishment.

Rosa's fingers bit into his arm.

"My God, it's Quelí and Greta Henry!" she gasped.
"They'll ride right into them and there's no way to warn
them!"

"We can try," Neville said grimly.

Towing the girl, he broke from cover into the open

again, running as fast as he could. When they were well into the clear they began waving their arms wildly as they ran. Neville knew that at this distance the human voice could not overcome the morning updrafts on these slopes but he shouted as loudly as he could, risking drawing the attention of the Johnny Blues as well.

However, their efforts were fruitless. The two horsewomen from the Corona were too intent on discovering the source of the gunfire they had heard to see the signals at the timber fringe above them, and Blair, Crane, and their Johnny Blues were too engrossed with their approaching quarry to have eyes for any other movement.

The two unsuspecting girls rode right in among the hidden riders before they were aware of the ambush. The trap was sprung swiftly. They were overpowered, quickly lashed into their saddles, and the reins of their horses taken on lead. In moments the cavalcade was on the move again, its prisoners in its midst.

In less than five minutes it vanished again into the draw from which it had emerged. Hunting had been good. Apparently Blair and Crane were satisfied. The next move would be up to Spencer Stanton. But there couldn't be any retaliation until he could be made to know what had happened. And that would take time. Agonizing time. Neville cursed his own utter helplessness. Blair was such a goddamned fool!

The same thought was in Rosa's mind.

"In the name of God, what will they do to them?" she asked.

"You ought to know," Neville said bleakly. "You had some experience when Blair captured you."

He started downslope in long, reaching, half-running strides. Almost sobbing, Rosa stumbled after him.

Chapter 15

Neville ran across the scuffed turf where the two Corona girls had been ambushed. A few yards further on was a high bank of outcropped clay and aggregate around which the now dry bed of a flood-stream washed in season. Beyond, sheltered from view from most directions, was a small cul-de-sac formed by erosion.

In the center of this lay the body of the Corona *vaquero*. Nearby were those of his horse and the steer he had been chousing along with his looped lariat. All had been cut down without warning by the single fusillade of shots he and Rosa had heard from higher ground.

It was an ugly sight. Neville turned back, intending to shield Rosa from it, but she was already upon him. She knelt beside the dead man and turned his face gently away from the crumple of his hat. She looked a long moment at the lifeless features and came slowly to her feet.

"Raúl Archuleta," she said softly. "One of the first Stanton *vaqueros*. Thirty years on the ranch. I've danced with his grandsons."

"I'm sorry."

She shook her head numbly.

"Now Quelí and Greta. Safe on Stanton land as they've always been. Not suspecting, no warning but those shots. Naturally they'd ride to see. Anyone on the ranch would. . . ."

She turned her face up to Neville.

"Why—what for—what can they hope to gain?" she demanded.

He shrugged heavily.

"You heard them. Crane and his renegades—money, I guess. Anything they can lay their hands on and get away clean. Blair—I don't know. I thought I did once. Some reasonable settlement with our father. With Tito and the rest. A fair one to all concerned when we'd made our point and proved we aimed to make it stick. Some kind of a place for us here. But by god not this!"

"We've got to get to Spencer Stanton."

"You do. Alone, from here on. I'm going after them while there's still a trail to follow. Before they do some senseless thing to that little half sister and her friend. Before they make it impossible to do anything but hunt them all down like mad dogs. Blair Stanton's still my brother—"

"You're as crazy as they are! What can you do afoot, crippled, with one bare hand? Come with me. We'll get help, attract attention, somehow. Maybe in only a few miles. You can make peace with your father, ride back with him and his crew. Tito, too. He'll show up. At least you'll be mounted and armed. . . ."

"Damn it, we're wasting time!" Neville flared angrily. "For chrissake, get started!"

He broke from her imploring grip so violently that she stumbled and fell to one knee. She looked up at him wide-eyed, startled by his anger. He guiltily stepped forward to help her up, but before he could give her his hand a voice rang out sharply behind him.

"Don't touch her again, you bullying bastard!"

Recognizing Tito Stanton's voice, Neville froze. Rosa lurched past him.

"Tito—Tito, no!" she cried. "You don't understand. We were on our way for help when we found Raúl. We were trying to decide what to do."

Neville turned slowly and carefully. Tito stood at the toe of the clay bank sheltering the cul-de-sac. His gun was lined at Neville's belly. Rosa reached him.

"We escaped from them last night, after you did," she continued swiftly. "We were heading for headquarters, for anyone who could get word to your father. We saw Raúl, then those men from Ojos Negros. Then they disappeared and we heard shots."

"I know," Tito said. "I was trailing you, trying to catch up. I had a glimpse of two more riders in closer here, below you."

"Quelí and Greta Henry, on one of their rides. Those men spotted them, too. We saw them spring their ambush. Back there on the other side of that bank. They made the girls go with them."

"I saw the tracks." Tito looked darkly at Neville as he hesitantly approached. "Get this. Anything happens to those girls you'll be the first to die."

He belted his gun and crossed swiftly to the body of his fallen *vaquero*. He stood motionlessly a moment, then bent and cut a length of rein from the bridle of the dead man's horse. He came back with this and took Rosa's elbow, steering her away.

"What's to decide, now? The dead will have to wait."

He turned the girl back around the clay bank toward the place where his sister and her companion had been captured. His horse was cropping near the patch of hoof-torn sod. He went to the animal and began shortening the stirrup leathers.

"It was my job," he told Rosa. "I aimed to do it my way. Keep Spence and Jaime and the hands out of it. Can't now. The bastards are gone. Safe to travel the road. Kill my horse if you have to but get to Spence as fast as you can."

Rosa nodded and turned to the horse. Neville stepped close to give her a hand and she swung up. She glanced uneasily from him to Tito. Tito ignored the plea in her eyes.

"They left gear and grub at the springs in the *malpaís*," he continued. "I think they'll hole up there to wait out the next move. I'll trail 'em to make sure."

He reached up and wrenched something from the fork of his saddle. Rosa bent suddenly to Neville. She pulled him against her knee and kissed him. For that moment her lips were soft and open, warm and ardent. Then Tito gave the horse a hard whack on the flank and she was gone, hammering away toward the stage road north. She did not look back.

Neville looked at Tito. He saw that what his half brother had tugged from his saddletree was his own missing hook. Tito tossed it to him, followed by the length of strap he had cut from the reins of the dead horse in the cul-de-sac.

"You can strip new lacings from that," Tito said. "Who took it from you—Crane?"

"Blair."

"Blood'll tell. I'll take those papers Rosa issued you in Santa Fe."

"I don't have them. Blair does." Neville hesitated. "Something you ought to know. Title was supposed to be in both our names. So we could deal with the old man together. Blair had Rosa issue them in his name alone. She told me last night."

"Real son of a bitch, isn't he? Now he's dealt you out. That it?"

"He thinks."

"You're lucky. Don't fight it. A lot I hold against you. Some I don't. You're a goddamn fool but you stood up for Rosa out there in the *malpaís*. You got her away, which is what I should have done first. Head back to the road and take it south as fast as you can hoof it.

"You ought to hit Mora in five or six hours. Sooner, if some of the crew happens to be working up at this end. Abelardo's foreman. Tell him who you are— what's up there. Tell him I said to stake you a horse and rig and a bait of grub. Then you pound ass the hell out of this country for good. Don't even *look* back. If I ever set eyes on you again you're going to have your piece of the Stanton ranch all right, permanently, about six foot by three."

"No," Neville said quietly. He got out his knife, opened its blade with his teeth, and squatted at his half brother's feet, clumsily trying to slice a lacing-string from the strip of rein. "You need help sooner than any can get here. I'm going with you. Or I'll follow. You can't stop me."

"Just what in hell do you think you can do?"

"Whatever has to be done."

"Whatever?"

Neville nodded, struggling one-handed with the knife and the strip of leather.

"Blair's my brother, but one of those girls they took is at least part way my sister, too," he said.

"One mistake and I'll kill you."

"I may get killed but you won't be the one who does it."

Tito Stanton stood looking down for a long moment, then dropped to his hunkers beside Neville.

"Here, goddamn it, let me do that."

He took the knife and quickly sliced the rein into strips. He picked up the hook and swiftly laced the leather strings into the gauntlet. Neville thrust the stump of his wrist into the leather. His half brother drew the lacing tight, returning his missing hand to him.

They rose to their feet together, two men opposed by nature and the course of events. Each took the other's measure in silence. It was Tito who spoke.

"Maybe I was right after all," he said quietly. "Maybe blood will tell—if you give it enough slack."

He drew an extra handgun he had thrust under his belt and dropped it into Neville's empty holster. Turning abruptly, he struck off at a quick, long-reaching stride.

Neville hurried after him, overtaking him in a few yards. They exchanged no glance but swung on wordlessly together in the tracks left by Blair Stanton and the renegade Johnny Blues with whom he now rode saddlemate.

Judging by the signs they left, their quarry rode without caution and in no great haste. They kept generally

to the open for easier going and seemed to be deliberately courting discovery by any others of the Corona
they might encounter, even at a distance. They held
steadily to the southeast and Neville had little doubt
that Tito was right: they were heading back into the
badlands to hole up in the security of Ojos Negros.

Tito continued to maintain a rapid pace. Boots, soft-
ened to the feet by long days in the saddle, chafed flesh
unaccustomed to the earth underfoot for any sustained
length of time. The sun climbed higher and the grass
began to thin out into the cinder-streaked soil marking
the onset of the *malpaís*.

Each tiny obsidian facet of fragmented lava reflected
the sun so that its effect was doubled. Neville became
increasingly aware of the heat and glare.

Tito unknotted the kerchief about his throat, shook it
out, and removed his hat. He spread the upper corners
of the square of cloth over his head above his ears.
When he replaced his hat to hold it, the kerchief hung
down from under the sweatband like a curtain to protect his cheeks, ears, and the back of his neck.

Neville did the same and found considerable immediate relief. The loose-hanging cloth warded off the heat
and yet allowed air to move freely beneath. It was, he
supposed, the same notion that had made Rosa Martinez bring Tito's blanket when they slipped away from
the main spring at Ojos Negros.

He wondered anew at this country and the people in
it. By his standards he was an intelligent and reasonably
well informed man. He had the advantages of a society
long skilled in defending itself against the dangers and
discomforts of its surroundings, wherever they might be.
His people had been impressing this knowledge for generations upon the less favored across half of the earth.

Yet from the first he had found himself unable to
cope with some of the most basic tenets of existence in
this high country. Here the solution of even simple daily
problems seemed to be guided by unspoken traditions
and foreknowledge far more ancient and more closely

related to the land itself than those upon which he had
been trained to rely.

Granted it was a hard country. A brutal one in many
respects. But it was kind to its own. It appeared to
speak with a voiceless tongue and those who listened
and understood profited by its counsel in myriad ways
beyond his comprehension. An instinct retained from
some immemorial time.

Perhaps it was this that made those born to the land
speak so warily of *extranjeros*—of outlanders in their
midst, unanointed, uninformed, and therefore suspect.
There was kinship here and deep loyalties but it was a
closed brotherhood and the opening difficult to find.

"You and Rosa saw them in the clear," Tito said
suddenly, as though their conversation had not been interrupted by an unbroken hour of silence. "How many
of them were there?"

"The lot, less the two whose heads you broke getting
away last night."

"No choice. They'd have given the alarm. Can't be
undone now. Means they picked up the three sentries I
disarmed and ordered to hell out. So that comes to
nothing. Can't afford another mistake like it. Spence'll
have my ass as it is."

"How long till he and your crew overtake us?"

Tito shrugged.

"Too damned long for us to wait and find out. If
they lay hand to Greta and Quelí—"

"I know. Quelí—curious name."

"Not hers. Spence gave it to her. For *qué linda*—
how pretty."

Neville sensed a more than fraternal pull of emotion
in Tito's voice.

"Her friend—" he said, "—Greta?"

"My *novia*."

"Fiancée?"

"We're not all that formal out here. It's just understood. My life. Let it go at that."

They slogged on in silence and presently came to a

small stream. It was already beginning to percolate away to nothing in the thickening volcanic ash through which it trickled. They watered upstream from the trampled puddling left by those they followed.

Tito rinsed out and replaced the kerchief hanging from under the sweatband of his hat. Neville sloshed his own head and neck with relish. Tito squatted beside him, waiting for him to swab up the excess.

"What happened with you and Rosa last night?" he asked. "That kiss when she left us. She doesn't whore around."

Neville bristled.

"She wasn't whoring. Neither was I. And nothing happened last night. In Santa Fe, maybe, first time we saw each other. Did to me. How the hell do I know about her? Wasn't for this damned thing—" he banged his hook against his knee, "I'd like to find out. And do something about it if I ever get the chance."

"Man never knows till he tries," Tito said. He rose to his feet. "How good do you shoot?"

"Lot of dead Yankees in Virginia aren't around to answer that any more."

"We're likely to find out. Let's get at it."

Chapter 16

Quelí Stanton was not frightened. She had not had a chance to warn Greta as to what had happened, what was happening. But she had known at once what the presence of these men meant.

'Mana had told her the true identity and intent of her half brothers soon after their departure from the Corona. Her mother had done so against her father's wishes, she was sure. Now they were back in defiance of Spencer Stanton. To what lengths they might go she could only guess. But she did not fear them.

Why should she? Fear had been something unknown in the great house on the Corona since earliest memory. She had grown up believing the Stantons impervious to it. Jaime Henry, too, and Raúl Archuleta and his boys and even crippled old Amelio, all those faithful friends whom she loved and respected.

How could she be different? Or Greta Henry, now riding white-faced and silent beside her. Or 'Mana or Helga Henry or Mama Archuleta and her daughters and granddaughters. They were Corona women. They could be no less fearless.

But she was shocked to the core of her being. She could not believe what was occurring. In some other time and place, maybe. She knew that greed and violence were abroad. Arrogant invasion, trampling of the rights of others, banditry and death, rape and theft and murder. Ruffians and renegades and rogues without decency or principle.

She had heard tales of Bloody Kansas and the Missouri Raiders. She knew of disorders in the California

gold fields and on the Nevada Comstock and in the
gaunt miners' mountains of Colorado. Travellers
brought frequent word of lawlessness flaring volcani-
cally in Apache Arizona and the bushwhacking war between opposing nationals that had never ended along
the Mexican border.

Those who lived on the Stanton ranch did not lead
such sheltered lives that they did not understand the
hatreds and ambitions spawned by the frontier of which
they were an inescapable part. They knew the nature of
restless men and women and the excesses of which
some were capable in times of provocation or mere opportunity.

Nowhere was the immutable pattern of life and death
more clearly drawn than on this high grass. That which
sprang from the earth must return to it. It was the first
law of nature. The strong must destroy the weak. This,
she thought, was the real source of her shock.

She watched Blair Stanton as they rode. He was a
handsome man, confident in his physical superiority.
Yet he was only half a Stanton as she knew Stanton
men. And the rest of his company, with the possible
exception of the one he called Crane, were common
dregs and drifters, a far cut below him.

It seemed incredible that such men could challenge
her father with such obvious confidence. She wondered
uneasily what secret knowledge they possessed, what
advantage or plan they had, to be so sure of success
against the most formidable adversary in New Mexico.

The Stanton ranch was as inviolable as her own per-
son. Guns now long silent and men now long dead had
carved that fact indelibly into the history of the Territory. All men knew this. Even the most violent and
reckless had learned to stay clear of all things marked
with the Corona crown.

Yet these renegades had boldly seized Spencer Stanton's and Jaime Henry's daughters in the very heart of
the ranch. It was an open and intentional invitation to
disaster and as such it made no sense. Whatever else,

she did not believe that the man riding at their head could be that much a fool.

She glanced at Greta Henry. Her *comadre* rode with the same tight-lipped expression and high lift of head that she did herself, but she sensed the same shock and utter disbelief in the older girl. Perhaps a trace of the fear that she denied as well. It was hard to know. Greta had her mother's eyes. For all their depth they could be as opaque as stone.

They came to a small stream on the edge of the *malpaís*. The party halted to water. By this Quelí judged their course beyond would lead into the arid and trackless badlands. This did not trouble her unduly.

Like most on the ranch, she had always avoided the lava as a hostile place, a confusing and unrewarding labyrinth in which the luckless could easily become lost. When this occasionally happened, it was usually only Lela who could find them.

Lela was one of Raúl Archuleta's daughters-in-law. She was a woman of the Utes and was known the length of the Sangre de Cristos as the finest tracker in all of the high country. Her trail sense was infallible. Quelí knew that when ranch headquarters discovered that she and Greta were missing, Lela would ride with the men. She always did when the need was to follow sign, however faint and cold.

Blair Stanton dismounted and came to Quelí's stirrup. He smiled pleasantly up at her. Too pleasantly.

"Comfortable?" he asked.

She remembered that this man and his brother had sat at her mother's table and slept in her father's house as guests, and she was a Stanton. She spat in his face. He flushed deeply, and then fastidiously wiped the spittle from his cheek with his kerchief. His expression did not otherwise change but she saw he would not forget.

He pointed to a small copse of brush downstream.

"In case you ladies wish—" he suggested.

Quelí looked at Greta and nodded. 'Mana had always taught her to avoid coping with more problems at one time than she had to. Certainly enough problems faced them now and there was no way to know when they might have as decent an opportunity to relieve themselves again.

Turning her horse to avoid the man at her stirrup, she stepped down. Greta joined her. They headed wordlessly toward the brush. Behind them they could hear both men and horses making water where they stood.

They wormed into the best shelter they could find in the thicket and squatted near each other for mutual reassurance. For the first time they could speak without betraying their anxieties to their captors.

"One of your half brothers, isn't he?" Greta asked. "The good-looking one."

Quelí nodded.

"Where's the other—with the hook?"

"Around. Got to be. He'll turn up."

"What do you think they intend to do with us?"

Greta's shoulders quivered with an involuntary shudder of aversion. Quelí understood and spoke quickly to discourage the thought.

"Not that. I don't think so. They wouldn't dare."

"They dared to capture us."

"For a good reason," Quelí agreed. "Somebody from the ranch. Maybe just whoever they could find. But if they touch either one of us it'll end their chances right then. They've got to know that."

"I wish I was as sure."

"There'd be no trading with my father or yours or Tito or any other man on the Corona after that. And I think that's what they want. To force a deal of some kind. Land, maybe, a share, like they wanted the first time they showed up. Or money—ransom or something."

"It'll be hours before they discover at the ranch that we're missing, let alone finding us. Maybe days—"

"Sooner than that," Quelí said with an assurance she did not feel. "Raúl Archuleta was somewhere down in those cutbanks below us. Those shots would have alerted him, too. Maybe he even saw what happened. Or read it from the ground. He's well on his way for help right now."

Greta shook her head accusingly.

"It's no use pretending, *comadre*. We both know it. They killed Raúl to keep him from doing just that—or trying to rescue us himself. That's what those shots were."

"Pray God they weren't."

"God forgive me but I'd rather pray to Spencer Stanton," Greta answered with her mother's bluntness, "and I hope to hell he hears in a hurry!"

Greta was about to add something else but broke off apprehensively at the sound of approaching footfalls. They stopped and a man hailed them from the edge of the thicket.

"Time enough. Come on or I'll come in after you."

The girls rose hastily and made their way through the brush. Crane was waiting for them in the open, a smirk on his face.

"You're learnin'," he said. "We'll have you halter-broke by nightfall."

He stood aside, forcing them to pass him, and brought up the rear. Quelí looked back and saw that his eyes were following the movements of their bodies with relish. There was no defense against this indignity but she grimly promised herself retaliation.

The men were already mounted. Crane moved toward Greta to give her a hand up but she was too quick for him, toeing her stirrup and pulling her horse in a tight turn toward her that swung her smartly into the saddle before he could reach her. Some of his comrades laughed at his discomfiture. Crane did not take it well.

He stepped to his own seat and reined to her.

"Don't put on no airs with me," he said. "Never was a filly I couldn't ride if I was of a notion."

Quelí kicked defensively up abreast of Greta. Blair Stanton came up outside of her and caught the cheek strap of her bridle, forcing her horse to accompany his and separating her from Greta.

"One big, happy family," he smiled. "Or will be when the old man's had time to come to his senses enough to be reasonable. Might as well get a little better acquainted. Besides, can't have you two plotting together behind our backs, can we?"

He glanced over his shoulder and his smile widened. He retained his grip on her bridle until he was satisfied she would keep her place beside him. She realized it was useless to attempt to avoid his proximity and made no effort to do so. He dropped his hand and settled comfortably in his saddle.

Quelí risked a glance behind her. Crane was riding stirrup-to-stirrup beside Greta, deliberately crowding in so close that their boots brushed. He was unabashedly watching Greta's full-bosomed bodice respond to the movement of horse and taking open pleasure from the effrontery. There was no help for this, either. Not now.

The rest of the troop was strung out behind, well satisfied with themselves and watching the byplay ahead with sardonic amusement. Much of Quelí's surety began to fade. This still could not be happening, but it was.

When she straightened in her saddle, Blair's eyes were upon her. He seemed to be reading her thoughts.

"So you understand—" he said, "you'll get exactly what you earn from us. Or what others earn for you. Spencer Stanton and brother Tito. It's up to you and them. Not us. The choice is yours—and theirs."

One word struck Quelí. Her mind raced with it. *Tito*. Blair's mention had been casual but in connection with her father. It was almost as though he assumed Tito was on the ranch and would act in concert with Spencer Stanton when it was learned she and Greta Henry had disappeared. It was even stronger than that. He believed this to be so.

Yet she knew her brother was in Santa Fe. He had been for several days, helping Saul Wetzel and Heggie

Duncan dig into a robbery at the Corona Guaranty and
Trust. She probed swiftly for clarification.

No. She was wrong. She didn't *know* Tito was in the
capital. Only that he had been, that as of breakfast this
morning he had not returned and was not expected. She
did not actually know where he was or where he might
be. It was therefore possible that Blair Stanton did.

It had been to Santa Fe that her father had directed
Blair and his brother when he ordered them off of the
Corona. The most likely place they could have recruited
the men now holding her prisoner was off the streets of
the old city. And they would have been there before
Tito. He could have encountered them, become suspicious of their intentions, and followed them when they
rode north again.

It was Tito's way, single-minded and single-handed.
She glanced back again to where Crane was pressing his
unwanted attentions on Greta Henry. A thin smile
pulled at Quelí's lips. If Tito Stanton was indeed back
on this side of the mountains, a reckoning was no further away than he was himself.

The thought was warm and welcome even if it was no
more than a vague hope with nothing to sustain it but
the inflection of a single spoken word. Few knew Tito
Stanton as his sister did. Not even 'Mana in all her gentle wisdom. Theirs was a wilder blood.

What her captors could not know was that if by some
miracle Tito showed up before this was done, she and
Greta would not only each have a vengeful father and
devoted friends to defend her; both would have Tito
Stanton as well. That was part of Stanton pride. She
unconsciously straightened in her saddle, her smile wid-
ening.

Her half brother misunderstood.

"Better," he said. "We'll get along."

"Don't count on it," she answered.

Quelí knew there was water in the *malpaís* but she
had never been to the low-walled compound at Ojos

Negros. The raiding party and its prisoners approached it from the north. There was no sign of life about the abandoned *jacals* within the enclosure. Gear scattered about betrayed occupancy, however, and Quelí knew that her captors were headquartered here.

They rode up to a crude gate in the wall and dismounted.

"Unsaddle and turn the stock out," Crane ordered. "It'll only get in the way here."

"Hold on a minute, Ted," a big, powerful man protested. "That just ain't good sense. We got to run them damned horses down afoot again, it'll sure put a crimp in us if we gotta clear outa here in a hurry!"

"No problem, Zep," Crane answered easily. "When we leave here we're goin' in style, full pockets and plenty of time to catch up, load our gear, and set our own pace. I want every gun emptied, cleaned, and recharged. I want every cap-box and shot-pouch and powder-flask filled. When company comes we're goin' to be ready for the bastards. They'll dance to our tune or there won't be no dancing."

The men fell to as ordered. Crane took Greta's elbow and steered her along the wall past the opening of the gate. Greta flinched at his touch but did not attempt to resist, accompanying Crane stiff-backed and haughty. Blair Stanton nodded approvingly.

"Good idea," he said.

He took Quelí's arm as well and propelled her after the other two.

A little beyond the gate the ashes of a dead fire were against the outside wall. On a blanket nearby the bodies of two men lay in the sun. The blood on their heads had not yet fully coagulated but both bodies were beginning to distend in the heat. Their captors forced the girls to the edge of the blanket.

One man's skull had been crushed by a single blow with some heavy instrument. Crane thrust out a boot and rolled the body of the other over. The face and forehead had been battered beyond recognition. He looked at the girls.

"So's you know this ain't no damned tattin' bee or a game of pinochle," he said. "Two of our best men. Buddies to some of the rest. They've took it some hostile."

He nodded toward the spotty grass threading off through the lava where the first of the freed horses was already beginning to roll off sweat and dust.

"Out yonder last night," he continued. "While the rest of us was right here in camp. Stantons done that. Your breed. No warning. No call, neither. Hard doings. We're doing as hard from here on. Any we can lay hands or sights to. Even you—both of you—if we have to."

He called to some men nearby and indicated the blanket on which the bodies lay.

"Drag 'em over to one of them potholes in the lava and dump 'em in. Toss some rocks on top to keep the flies and coyotes off."

Two men took up the ears of the blanket and dragged it and its burden off toward the nearest tongue of lava. Greta closed her eyes and turned away. Quelí looked at Blair Stanton. His face was expressionless. There was no aversion, no remorse in his eyes. Only a high, glinting excitement she had seen before when *vaquero* stakes ran high at cards in one of the *casitas* in the adobe village below the Corona house.

Blair met her look with a shrug.

"Not pretty, but he means it," he said. "So do I, if it comes to that. I tried to tell you. We've tried to tell them. We left one of their riders dead behind us when we jumped you out there this morning. Believe me, the only way's whatever influence you have with your father and brother when they show up."

It was Quelí's turn to momentarily close her eyes. So Greta had been right about Raúl Archuleta, after all. No prayers could undo that, now. And no prayers would be a comfort here. She reopened her eyes and spoke levelly.

"My father and brother aren't women. They don't deal with women when their business is with men."

"We'll see," Blair answered.

He turned her back to the gate and through it. Crane and Greta moved with them. They started across the compound toward the best-preserved of the *jacals*. Quelí saw that as crude as the enclosure was the place was a potential fortress. A few could stand off many indefinitely here.

Crane indicated the *jacal* ahead and jogged Blair with his elbow.

"Your brother must be sleepin' in," he said jocularly. He ran his eyes appreciatively over Greta's figure again. "Can't say I blame him, the bedfellow we left with him. Beats poundin' ass in a saddle."

They reached the door of the stone hut and stepped into the gloom within. It was without furnishings and unoccupied. The two men stared in astonishment.

"Son of a bitch!" Crane breathed. "Gone—the both of 'em!"

"How the hell could they be?" Blair protested. "No guns, horses—anything."

"You even took the bastard's hook."

Blair nodded, eyes searching in disbelief.

"So his gut was in an uproar when we left, Neville'd still have better sense than to set off across the lava afoot at night."

"I'd say so," Crane agreed. "Specially with a gal you'd already pretty well used up, tryin' to get the truth or whatever out of her."

Blair's grip on Quelí's arm suddenly tightened.

"It's that goddamned Tito!" he said. "He doubled back and got them after we cleared out. Look! He stole one of our saddles when he sneaked off because he couldn't get his own out of this shack without attracting attention. It's gone now. He slipped back, made the trade, and took Neville and the girl with him."

"Looks like it. Damned if it don't," Crane agreed. A suspicion glinted in his eyes. "Your brother may a gone willing, what with the shine he took to that little bitch from Santa Fe and the run-in he had with you. If he did, we maybe got something of a problem on our hands, Stanton."

Blair freed Quelí's arm and turned sharply on Crane. Quelí sensed the underlying tension between the two.

"No," he said harshly. "Not one that wouldn't have to be settled anyway. Get this straight and quit pussy-footing around it, Crane! Neville's already made his bed. Let him lie in it."

"I got to be sure."

"I'm telling you. There's no room for him at the end of the line. Never has been. Just you and me. You and me and every drop of blood we can squeeze out of Spencer Stanton."

"Christ, man, he's your brother!"

"And the old man's my father," Blair countered. He jerked his head at Quelí. "She's my sister. What the hell difference does that make as long as we get what we want? A goddamned fortune. The old man can raise it and he will. That's what counts. It's all that does."

Crane shook his head in canny, grudging admiration.

"You're a rotten bastard," he said.

"Two of a kind, Crane. And we've got work to do. Word's sure as hell got to the ranch now. They're long on their way. We'd better be ready for them."

Crane released Greta with a glance of regret and strode out. Blair followed. He turned in the doorway.

"Stay here," he ordered the girls. "Keep out of sight. One of you shows herself, she's going to damned well wish she hadn't!"

Chapter 17

The heat grew more oppressive. Neville's mouth dried and his lips began to cake as the thin, dry air sucked all moisture from them. Breathing became painful. Still Tito maintained their pace unslackened. Grateful for his own foresight, Neville unslung the canteen he had brought from the *jacal* at Ojos Negros and offered it. Tito declined with a shake of his head. Pride made Neville sling the canteen back across his shoulder, its stopper untouched.

For the thousandth time he craned back over his shoulder in search of hard-riding horsemen on their back-trail but he saw only the endless, empty expanse of the *malpaís*. The glassy black rock underfoot had worn through the sole of one boot. He was beginning to limp painfully. His attention diverted by his backward look, he stumbled and half-fell. An obsidian shard slashed his knee and he grunted involuntarily at the bite.

"Not time enough yet," Tito said without turning his head. "Best watch where you're going. You know where you've been and there's more ahead."

They slogged on. Neville searched the tormented skyline of the badlands for some formation he could recognize that might tell him how far they were from the springs in the lava. But for all their diversity, there was a frustrating monotony to the low buttes of the flows. To his unpracticed eye all looked hopelessly the same.

Tito carried the rifle he had pulled from his saddle with Neville's hook. He passed it occasionally from hand to hand to distribute the burden. Otherwise his attention remained riveted on the ground before them.

Occasionally he changed course slightly as the signs of passage he followed indicated.

Neville thought it was nearing midafternoon when Tito pulled up. The sheer black wall of a flow faced them. It loomed fifty or sixty feet above the ancient level on which they stood.

"Springs're in another slot like this on the other side," Tito said. "Half a mile or so.".

Neville looked at the bare furnace rock above them, table-flat and without growth. No longer able to resist, he pulled the canteen around and sucked at its neck. The water lubricated his tongue and restored his voice. Tito reached out his hand. Neville passed the canteen to him and looked at the flow again.

"We'll have to find a way around," he said. "We go over, they'll see us the minute we're on top."

Tito rinsed out his mouth and spat away the residue.

"Will anyway, any direction we come, the way the flows lie," he said. "Unless we can go under."

"Under?"

"Maybe with luck I can show you. It's worth the time to try."

Leaving the sign they had been following for the first time, Tito started along the base of the flow, searching the face above them. In little time he spotted the darker slash of a fissure in the lichen-spotted stone. They climbed to it. The opening would barely admit a man.

"This may set us back a hell of a ways," Tito said. "But with just the two of us, we've got to catch 'em by surprise or we're helpless, anyways. Odds're better'n six to one as it is. Can't get much worse. Willing to chance it?"

Neville nodded wordlessly.

Tito handed him the rifle and lowered himself feet first into the fissure. He dangled there a moment, head and shoulders at surface level.

"When you let go, fall limp," he said. "May be quite a drop. Sometimes these tubes are pretty big. Twenty feet or so."

Neville nodded again. Tito let himself go and plummeted from view. Neville heard him strike the bottom. In a moment his voice floated up, reverberating as though from the bowels of the earth.

"We're in luck. Looks like a good one. And there's more light than usual. Drop the rifle and come on."

Neville held the rifle over the fissure and let go. He heard the slap of Tito's hands as he caught it. He lowered himself into the hole, astonished to feel a cool underground wind rushing out past him. He hung suspended for a moment, then dropped.

He landed joltingly but without mishap about ten or twelve feet below. Light from the fissure overhead revealed Tito facing him on the floor of a curious, tunnel-like cavern that stretched darkly away into the distance as far as he could see. The walls, floor, and overhead, each curving into the other in a perfect cone like the inside of some huge pipe, were as smooth as if cut by a giant drilling machine and seemed to be lined with dark, molten glass.

Tito smiled briefly at his astonishment.

"Something, eh? Saul Wetzel read up on 'em when Spence took him into one out here years ago. According to him they aren't sure what causes 'em but they think that when a flow starts to cool the core remains liquid for a while. Sometimes a leak develops and the core drains out before it's had a chance to set.

"Leaves these tubes. Later the outer crust breaks through, like the way we got in. Lets light in, too. Saul says some places they run for miles. Not here. Guess old Fire Mountain didn't have enough guts to spew out for that. But if this one holds direction maybe we can get a little closer to Ojos Negros without being seen."

"Suit me to come out right under their feet. Better footing than the weathered stuff outside."

"Yeah, well, I doubt we've lived good enough lives for that kind of luck. Let's play the hand as it is."

Tito started off through the dimly lit gloom. It grew darker and more sepulchral as the fissure by which they had entered fell away behind them. Then a fresh source of light began to glow ahead. The tube bent and turned, its floor undulating with the original surface over which the lava had flowed.

They passed another pile of rubble where the outer shell had given away to weathering and a section had tumbled in. Handing Neville the rifle, Tito scrambled up the heap to the opening and peered out.

"Gaining," he called down. "Shall we push our luck a little more?"

"Long as it holds," Neville agreed.

Tito rejoined him and they moved on. Light fell away behind them again until the darkness became almost total and they had to feel their way along the smooth, glassy wall. Finally they could no longer see even a pinpoint of light from the last fissure they had passed. With the outer world utterly sealed off the silence was eerie.

Tito halted and Neville ran into him.

"I don't know," Tito said. "Long way back to that last hole already. We go on we may just be making more trouble for ourselves."

Neville located a chunk of stone with his reaching toe and flung it as hard as he could into the darkness ahead of him. It struck a spark in the distance and went clattering on down the tube a hundred yards or so by the time it took to finally come to rest. The echoes of its clatter persisted for several seconds more before finally dying out.

"Let's try it a bit further," he said.

Tito resumed and Neville followed, guiding themselves by the sidewall as before. Presently the floor began to take a definite downward slant. Tito stopped again.

"Every foot we go down's a foot we got to climb if we have to go back," he said. "And we're taking the risk of a drop-off any time."

He flung another fragment of rock ahead. It skipped away noisily down the tube and came to rest.

"All right," he said when silence returned, "time's worth the gamble."

They moved cautiously forward again. Twice more Tito tested the way with a flung stone. Then, suddenly, Neville was aware that Tito was becoming a faint silhouette before him. The tube bent and a tiny, bright point of light hung distant in the darkness.

"Jackpot!" Tito chuckled. "Reckon one of us has lived a cleaner life than I thought, after all."

They hurried on, breaking into a jog in their eagerness as the light grew and they could see their footing.

The new fissure proved to be very small and directly overhead. The surrounding lava was badly fractured for some distance around it but the actual opening was no larger than a man's head, far too small to admit his body. So little debris had fallen from it that even standing on the rubble they could not reach the aperture, let alone climb into it.

Disappointed, they resumed. A few yards further on the tube bent again and petered out against a wall of ancient slag.

"Shit!" Tito said for them both.

Heavy-footed, they retraced their steps. Tito halted under the little overhead fissure through which daylight poured. He studied it thoughtfully then set the rifle aside.

"Give me a lift up," he said, then realized that with his handicap Neville could not do what he asked. "Damn it, I forgot. Look, my flask's full of powder. Plenty to do us both if need be. Take yours. Wedge it into that biggest crack up there as deep as you can. Leave the lid open and see if you can crimp a cap into the hinge or something so it'll stay and I can see it from down here."

He laced the fingers of both hands together and Neville stepped into them. Tito stood rock-steady under the weight, supporting Neville easily. The powder-flask fit easily into the big crack and wedged firmly. Neville placed a percussion cap so that its business end pointed into the open neck of the flask.

Tito lowered him and he stepped down. They backed off a ways until the cap at the neck of the wedged flask became an impossibly tiny target. Neville could see no hesitation or evidence of concentration as Tito swung the rifle up. It seemed to fire while its sights were still in motion but the cap flashed and the powder exploded.

In this restricted place the report of the weapon and the makeshift blasting charge were mere thuds, one heavier than the other, rather than the explosions Neville expected. Dust flew, spalls of shattered stone ricocheted from the walls, and a great chunk of the overhead came down heavily in a mass of rubble. It revealed a crooked chimney rising through a dozen feet of weathered rock to a patch of sky twice that size across.

Tito grinned but he methodically reloaded the discharged rifle before he stirred from his tracks.

"One of the first things Spence taught me," he said. "He wouldn't carry an unloaded gun across a room. Says it's like packing a dead body—no use to anyone, least of all its owner."

Neville climbed first into the chimney, finding hand-and footholds in its broken walls. In this his hook was more useful than hand and fingers. The sharp curved steel wedged easily and firmly into the broken stone.

He emerged in a shallow little depression on the flat cap of the flow. He thought that storm water gathering in this had slowly percolated into the lava and had rotted out the original fissure they had opened up. He reached down for the rifle and Tito followed, joining him.

Neville couldn't tell how far they had come or how much they had benefited their position, if at all, but Tito seemed to know precisely where they were.

"Couldn't be better," he said. "Now we'll see what we can do about really frying those bastards' *cojones* for 'em!"

He led off, heading directly for the edge of the flow. From here they had an overview of one of the tongues of grass watered by the springs. Recently released horses, yet dark-patched with sweat, were rolling and nuzzling on it. They found a way down the face of the flow to the lower level and followed the base of the spur of lava through which they had passed to its tip.

At this point they found themselves separated by only a few hundred yards of broken field chunks of solidified lava spewed out by Fire Mountain from the rough wall surrounding the *jacals* at the main spring. Blair and Crane had ordered all their horses turned loose. None were at the wall or within the enclosure.

There was no sign of Quelí Stanton or Greta Henry but preparations for a siege were obvious. Crane's men were stationed along the wall at intervals, heads appearing here and there as they shifted position to make themselves more comfortable and secure. Tito nodded with satisfaction.

"We're some east of where they'd expect us or anybody from the ranch to show up, so they won't watch so sharp in this direction," he said. "And we saved ourselves a hard hour of climbing and belly-crawling by taking a chance on that tube. But we got to work closer."

"Only one thing bothers me, Tito," Neville admitted. "If those from the ranch are following us, we lost them when we dropped in that hole. How we going to link up when they get here?"

"Time enough to worry about that when they do," his half brother answered. "Right now we're going to try to close in. Watch those Johnny Blues a bit."

Neville did. He had a glimpse of Blair at the wall near the gate. A few moments later Crane appeared briefly at the corner of the *jacal* in which they had held Tito and Rosa Martinez prisoner. He judged that this was also where Quelí and Greta Henry were being held, hidden from sight and hopefully safe from harm. The rest of the men were minding their own positions.

"Man thinks he's a herd animal but he isn't," Tito said. "A hell of a long way from it. Ever watch a bunch

of pronghorns or a flock of birds? Each individual
minds his own feeding or whatever, like there wasn't a
danger in a million miles. But there's always one that's
on guard and he really works at it. On a hummock or a
tree or someplace he can see in all directions. If there's
something suspicious he signals at the first sign. The
rest count on that.

"Look yonder. Every man-jack keepin' his own
watch. Because each one knows the others are too, nobody really covers the ground. Responsibility isn't
theirs, only a part of it. So they don't take it really to
heart. I'm going to make a spurt for that first rock.
Once I'm down behind it and settled and you don't see
any faces turned this way for a minute, you try for the
next beyond it."

Neville nodded. A moment later Tito was up and
gone, running bent and close to the ground, trailing his
rifle. Two dozen swift strides and he was down again
behind the rock he had selected from the scatter separating them from the wall of the enclosure about the
jacals. He looked back expectantly. Neville could see no
questing faces along the enclosure turned fully toward
him.

Bunching his feet beneath him, he lunged from cover
and sprinted as Tito had done, keeping to low silhouette. He passed Tito's position and sprawled down behind another shelter a few yards further on. Raising his
head cautiously, he saw with satisfaction that he had not
been seen at the *jacals*.

A few more moments of tense waiting ensued, then
Tito shot past him and flopped down behind another
big hunk of the scattered, broken fieldstone lava. Again
the movement went unnoticed in the enclosure. Leap-
frogging each other in this way when opportunity afforded, in a few minutes they cut the distance to the
lava wall behind which Crane and Blair and their renegades were forted to less than sixty yards. And it was all
open. No closer approach could be made.

Tito signalled Neville up beside him at his last position. Neville risked this final sprint and joined him. They could hear the occasional sound of voices at this range although the words could not be understood. Blair was still moving from position to position along the wall, checking each and making a change here and there. Ted Crane was squatting against the shady-side wall of the *jacal* in which they believed the prisoners were being held and only a few feet from the doorway.

Tito studied the enclosure for two or three minutes, then shifted position a little and studied all other potential approaches through the lava tongues with equal care. Finally he hunched back to Neville.

"Two belt-guns and a rifle," he said softly. "Thirteen shots. And I make twelve of them in there. One to spare. That's all we've got. So they've got to count, every damned one. Don't forget."

He drew his own gun—the lighter, beautifully hand-worked Navy Colt Neville had noted and handled once before. Tito began to remove and replace the caps to be sure they were rightly seated, meticulously wiping each nipple clean as he did so.

"When Spence and Jaime and the boys show up," Tito continued, "they'll come roarin' hell-for-leather out of one of those slots yonder, straight across that open grass for the wall. That's their way. And they'll be sitting ducks till they can jump it and get in hand-to-hand."

Neville began to check his own gun, realizing the wisdom of the precaution.

"It may not come to that," he said. "What with the girls here. Blair and Crane are counting on the old man to dicker to keep from risking them."

"Well, he won't. And don't call him that. We've got to give him cover as he comes in, make as big a diversion as we can. It's going to be some hairy, but the best way's to charge right into them from here before he's in range and they can cut down on him from cover. Surprise'll be with us but that's all. You game for it?"

"I said 'whatever' when I came with you," Neville answered. "As long as those girls are in there."

"That's the other thing," Tito said. "I'll snap-shoot better'n you. And that's what it'll be. On a dead run. I'll nail as many as I can as fast as I can. Don't you hunt targets. You get to that *jacal* before any of them can. In case I can't. Don't let a single one of those bastards get to those girls. Spence and Jaime and the boys'll handle the rest once they're over the wall."

Tito fell silent a moment, studying Neville. His face winced in a little grimace and he stretched out his hand for the belt-gun Neville was checking. Wondering, Neville surrendered it to him. Tito thrust it under his own belt and handed over the rifle with its single charge.

"You're going to have to do it with this," he said apologetically. "Way it is, we can't afford your wasting more than one shot in that first hard minute."

Protest surged up in Neville but he recognized Tito's painful honesty and the simple truth he stated. As they said in this country, that was the way it was.

"All right," he answered quietly. "Whatever."

Chapter 18

The afternoon was interminable. Quelí and Greta could sense restless movement about the compound. Frequently Blair Stanton's voice drifted to them as he talked with Crane's men, giving orders where he thought necessary.

Crane himself came once into the *jacal* with a canteen of water. His eyes said it was for Greta. He would have lingered, ignoring Quelí's presence completely, but Blair appeared suddenly in the doorway. He said nothing but the warning in his expression was plain enough. Crane bristled defensively.

"This goddamn waitin' grates on me," he said. "Just killin' a little time is all. Seein' to our guests. No harm in that."

Blair merely summoned him with a jerk of his head. Crane went reluctantly. As they moved away the girls could hear their voices, held low but mingled in hot argument.

"I'm afraid of him," Greta confided. "He's working himself up to something. If Tito was here last night like they said, where the devil is he now? It's not like him to let enemies out of his sight or give them a moment's peace while they're still on his land."

"No man's land out here," Quelí answered. "Not that it makes any difference. Don't worry, *comadre*. Tito'll be along directly. They all will."

Greta nodded soberly.

"That's something else I've been thinking about. What happens to us then? You know my father, yours, most of all Tito. They won't stop to parley like those *cabrones* think. They'll come roaring in shooting and be damned. Kill or be killed. If your half brother and the rest of these pigs are going to use us it'll be then. When the shooting starts. When they realize it's their last chance—their only one."

Quelí knew Greta was right. She had nursed the same thought but had not wished to further disturb Greta with it. However, it seemed wise to face it now.

"Then we'll have to take care of ourselves until they can get to us," she said matter-of-factly.

She had earlier noted for this very purpose a scatter of smoke-blackened, fist-sized stones half buried in one corner. She supposed they had once formed a chimney-less makeshift fire-space for use in inclement weather. She dug out two with her fingers and handed one to Greta.

"This do for a start?"

Greta weighed the stone approvingly.

"For a start," she agreed. "Let's dig some more out, ready to hand. Makes me feel better knowing there's at least something we can do if it comes to it."

Quelí nodded. She had never subscribed to the idea of a woman's helplessness. Another heritage from 'Mana's people, she supposed, mothers and daughters who had lived for generations with the realities of this land and learned to survive its hardships.

She found a chink in the rough wall of uncut and unmortared lava that would support the stone. It was inconspicuous and in easy reach at shoulder height. Greta found a similar place for the stone Quelí had handed her.

In twenty minutes they each selected half a dozen such weapons, earnestly discussing which were best for their purposes and the wisest places to cache them about the room. The task improved their spirits and soon they were smiling at their own earnestness.

"Cave women," Greta said as she scrubbed soot from her hands on the underside of the flare of her riding skirt. "Be almost a pity to not have to use at least a couple of them after this. Believe me, I'd sure as hell like to. On that one *torón,* anyway."

Suddenly her smile froze and she came slowly, tensely to her feet. Quelí spun toward the doorway. Crane was there. He looked furtively back into the compound then stepped quickly inside. His lips drew back in a smile in which there was no humor.

"Either one of you opens her mouth I'll knock her teeth in," he said without particular malice. He gestured Quelí toward a corner with an additional blunt warning. "Keep out of this or I'll see you do."

Quelí backed slowly against the wall, her hand fumbling behind her for one of the loose stones they had spaced along it. Crane advanced unhurriedly on Greta.

"No real harm," he said. "Just a little friendliness. For appearances, hunh? Something to cool their piss off if Old Man Stanton and that fast-gun kid of his don't want to listen to reason when they show up. High-ridin' blue-balls like that may take a little convincing we mean business—"

He reached out suddenly with both hands, before she could anticipate his intention, and caught Greta's bodice at the shoulders. He gave a violent tug downward. Seams parted at the yoke, fabric ripped, and the forepart of the garment came away, exposing much of her upper body.

"Now, by god, that's something!" Crane said with satisfaction, and he reached for the bared flesh.

Quelí's frantically searching fingers found the stone they were seeking and closed convulsively over it. She flung it as hard as she could. At the same moment Greta caught one of the man's reaching hands, bent to it, and sank her teeth into the ham of the thumb.

Crane doubled with a grunt of pain to free himself and Quelí's stone struck him higher on the head than she intended. It was no more than a glancing blow and drew no blood but it shook and further infuriated him. Quelí slid swiftly along the wall in search of another cached stone.

Crane brutally forced Greta's jaws apart to free his bleeding hand and flung her back against the wall so hard that she sagged there against it, momentarily half stunned. Quelí found another stone. Crane saw her as she turned with it.

He leaped for her and caught the swinging arm at the wrist. His grip closed so tightly and agonizingly that the stone fell helplessly from her fingers. He jerked her around and smashed the back of his bleeding hand angrily across her face, mingling his blood with her own.

Salt taste was in her mouth. Her knees loosened. She tried to cry out but could not. The blow came again, swinging from the other direction. It snapped her head back with its force. The room reeled and she dropped. He freed his grip and let her fall limply into the rubble underfoot.

She crouched there, supporting herself with her hands, shaking her head to clear it. She realized Crane had turned back to Greta. Her *comadre*'s breath caught in a sob of hurt and outrage and there were the sounds of a scuffle. Then Greta's voice rose in a scream of fury, ringing loudly in the confines of the *jacal*.

"You filthy son of a bitch!"

Quelí lunged unsteadily to her feet and lurched blindly toward the sound. She collided with the struggling bodies and grappled at the man, tearing at his shirt, clawing at anything to which she could set fingers and nails. He tried to fling her off but she clung tenaciously.

Then there seemed to be two of them and she was struggling with both. The hard bulk of a holstered gun banged against her thigh. She tried for the weapon. It came partially clear, then was torn from her grasp and fell underfoot as its wearer twisted defensively. Hands gripped her shoulders and shook her roughly. She heard Blair Stanton's voice.

"Stop it, damn it! It's all right, now—"

Reason returned and with it vision. Greta, heaving with outrage and exertion, was backed against the wall of the hut, trying to cover herself with her torn bodice. Crane was standing a yard away, his bitten thumb still dripping, his face nail-marked and also oozing. It was her half brother's hands that had gripped Quelí's shoulders.

Blair's handsome face was also deeply scratched. She realized the marks were those of her own nails. She felt a moment of contrition. He had come to their rescue at Greta's scream. In her own dazed fury she had not understood his intent or even been clearly aware of his presence.

The tail of Blair's shirt had been ripped out from under his belt half the way around his body and she saw that one of her hands was still tightly wound into it. He freed her grip. Blair's hands fell from her shoulders and she stepped back.

Only then did Quelí see that the eyes of the others had suddenly riveted on something at her feet. She looked down. Blair's gun lay trampled in the dirt where it had fallen when she half drew it from his holster and then lost it in the blind frenzy of her struggle. Partly atop it lay an oilskin packet securely tied with a thong.

A foot away was a hard-used makeshift belly-pouch of the kind frequently favored by travellers for their valuables. Its flap had burst open and minted gold spilled from it. Quelí realized both packet and pouch had spilled from Blair's shirt in his struggle with her.

There was a dreadful moment of sudden silence that Quelí knew was of great significance to the two men facing each other. Blair's face had paled to marble. Very slowly he bent to retrieve his belongings.

Crane took a step forward and planted his foot on the gun and packet, pinning them down before Blair's outstretched hand could reach them. Down on one knee, Blair looked up at him. A plea was in his eyes but he did not voice it. Without understanding but with a sense of horror, Quelí watched Crane unhurriedly draw and cock his gun.

With the muzzle of the weapon a scant foot from the

paled and handsome features, Crane fired it into Blair's face and continued to fire into the sprawled body until the gun's chambers were emptied.

Tito and Neville Stanton kept low in their cover. Blair was hunkered down out of their line of sight with two Johnny Blues stationed near the gate in the enclosure at Ojos Negros.

For some minutes Ted Crane had been idling near the *jacal* in which they believed the two girls from the Corona were being held. To all appearances he was merely keeping to the welcome shade cast by the hut. But now he had begun inching furtively along the wall of the *jacal* toward the door.

Near this he paused warily to shoot a quick look toward Blair's position. Apparently satisfied that his movement was not noted, he stepped quickly from sight through the opening.

"Bastard!" Tito hissed.

Neville nodded. Their tenseness grew. No sound came from the *jacal*, no evidence of trouble within. Seconds ticked away. Slowly both Tito and Neville began to ease. Then what both feared came—a shrill feminine scream, quavering with loathing and fury. The words carried clearly to them:

"You filthy son of a bitch!"

Every head in the enclosure jerked toward the *jacal*. Hidden men surged partially up from cover in startled curiosity. Blair lunged into view where he had been hunkered and sprinted hard for the hut.

Others would have followed him. He angrily waved them back to their stations as he ran. Tito stiffened ironhard beside Neville.

"No waiting now!"

He leaped into the clear, drawing his holstered gun and the spare in his belt as he moved, and raced for the enclosure wall fifty yards away. Clutching the rifle, Neville plunged after him, noting as the distance narrowed that in spite of his tenderfooted lameness he was the faster on his feet.

When they were barely halfway across to the wall, Blair reached for the door of the *jacal* beyond and dived within. Neville drew abreast of Tito. His half brother showed no awareness of his presence. Tito had become a finely honed machine, operating at top speed and efficiency for one purpose only and with no attention to waste on any distraction.

His breath came in audible grunts with the tremendous effort he was putting into each swiftly reaching stride. His eyes were straight ahead. The mismatched guns in his hands were rocking as though already paced by the recoil of exploding caps and powder. When gunsound came Neville thought for an instant that Tito had opened fire at unseen targets but the reports came from within the *jacal*, half a dozen shots loosed in an unhurried, rhythmic drumroll.

This fusillade even more tightly riveted the attention of the defenders of the compound upon the stone hut into which Crane and Blair Stanton had disappeared. The two newcomers running in from the lava-studded grass were not seen until they reached the wall and vaulted over it side by side.

While he was in midair Neville saw a white band of hatless forehead beneath him as one of the defenders jerked around in astonishment.

"What the hell!" a disembodied voice yelled hoarsely.

The man swung his gun up. Neville smashed down hard with the butt of the rifle but his leap carried him too far and he stumbled trying to recover. He knew as he rolled that he was a fair target but a gun slammed beside him and the menacing forehead vanished in a welter of red.

Neville regained his balance and raced on toward the *jacal*. Tito, one of his guns now smoking, cut at right angles behind him and ran parallel to the inner side of the enclosure wall, recklessly exposing himself but forc-

ing defenders there to show themselves for their chance
at him.

It was incredible gun work. Both of Tito's weapons
were now firing, shifting targets so swiftly that it seemed
impossible such marks could be hit, but he left none on
their feet behind him. Firing was now general, filling
the air with concussion and the angry whine of mis-
shapen lead whanging away from glassy black stone.

Once again Neville Stanton felt sensations he had
sworn to forget and never know again—the numbing
combination of deep gut-fear and the wild, eerie, mind-
less exhilaration he had known in battle. The curious
hallucinations of men at war. A strange conviction that
this instant in time was frozen for that interminable
aeon before death released it and set it in motion again.

The dark rectangle of the *jacal* doorway, still a tantalizing few yards away, seemed an objective impossible
to attain. God knew what lay beyond it. A bullet from
an unseen source struck the forepiece of Neville's rifle,
knocking him to one knee.

He saw Tito also go down. A Johnny Blue leaped out
from the rocks of the enclosure wall, his clubbed rifle
upraised in a powerful backswing. Twisting awkwardly,
Neville swept his own weapon around, leading his target
as he would the bulletlike flight of a jumped quail, and
loosed the one shot he had been allotted.

In spite of Tito's fear that the charge might be
wasted, the heavy, rifled slug took the charging man
with the clubbed rifle through the body from the pit of
one upraised arm to the other. The Johnny Blue spilled
across Tito, who struggled clear and regained his feet,
dragging one a little as he closed relentlessly with another defender among the rocks of the wall.

Neville scrambled up himself. A man appeared at the
corner of the *jacal* as he drove again toward the hut.
The man had a fair shot at him and took it but he allowed himself to be a little hurried. The bullet struck
Neville high in the shoulder of his good arm, flinging

him back on his heels, and the now useless rifle spilled from his shock-slackened grasp.

He regained his balance and lunged unsteadily on. The Johnny Blue, his own weapon now discharged, panicked back out of sight. Neville risked a backward glance. Tito took another bullet at the wall, shot a man through his own powdersmoke, and swung toward another he had flushed from cover. His extra pistol misfired or the hammer fell on an exploded cap.

Without breaking the ragged rhythm of his swing, Tito flung the gun at his intended target. The weapon caught the man full in the face with lethal force and he went down. Tito wheeled and reeled toward the *jacal* after Neville.

Suddenly the doorway of the *jacal* yawned before Neville and he plunged through it. A stark tableau faced him in the dark interior, another motionless instant frozen in time. Quelí Stanton, pinched-face pale and dazed with shock, cringed against the far wall. Beside her, dress badly torn, huddled a slightly older girl who Neville knew must be her friend, Greta Henry. Both were quick-breathing as though from struggle but neither appeared to have been seriously harmed.

Ted Crane, his heavy, insensitive face nail-scarred and twisted in fury and one thumb dripping blood, rocked on his feet in the center of the hut. All three seemed oblivious to the sudden salvo of gunfire in the enclosure outside. At the moment of Neville's entry their attention was riveted on the bullet-torn body of a man sprawled at Crane's feet.

It was Blair. He had been shot in the face at close range and his lifeless body pumped full of lead. Beside him lay his own gun, the packet that contained the map of the *malpaís* and the deed from Santa Fe, and the gold-spilling belt-pouch he had stolen from Crane in Glorieta Pass. As Neville had warned, this last had been Blair's death warrant.

Chapter 19

As Neville's figure dimmed the light from the doorway, the tableau within the *jacal* shattered. Quelí Stanton cried out in recognition or warning. He was not sure which. The eyes of the two girls shot fearfully to Ted Crane. The ex-sergeant grunted with the fury that still gripped him.

"You, too, by god!" he swore.

He slanted up the gun that had been dangling limply in his uninjured hand but he flung it from him as though realizing it was discharged and dived for Blair's weapon in the dirt of the floor. Neville's unchecked momentum carried into the man with an impact that sent a shaft of breath-catching pain through the numbness in his wounded shoulder.

There was no animus in him, no sense of obligation and duty. That had died at the sight of the imprisoned girls unharmed. But the bullet-torn body on the cinders underfoot had been his brother. Crane had killed him. Whatever the justification, many recollections of excitement and danger had ended here. Many miles of shared trails through the years. Only this was in Neville's mind as he bowed his back and heaved up mightily with his hook before Crane's scrabbling fingers reached Blair's gun.

The hook caught Crane under the chin and set deeply as Neville's bent body snapped erect. The man's head jerked back and he was hoisted almost to his feet before he fell away backward. The hook held, almost pulling Neville after the falling man, so deeply was it embedded. Then it wrenched free, the sharp, pointed steel bringing the gullet with it. Crane made no sound and was dead when his shoulders hit the floor.

Neville knelt and tried to retrieve Blair's belongings from the cinders, but the bloody hook was not equal to the task in his present state. Quelí Stanton and Greta Henry seemed to understand his wishes and, resolutely turning their backs on the ghastly ruin he had made of Crane's throat, they bent to help him.

Blair's gun was dropped into his own empty holster. They handed him the packet of papers from Santa Fe and replaced the gold spilled from Crane's belt-pouch and gave him this, also. He clamped these under his arm, still not trusting himself to work the gripping device on the hook. One to either side, they helped him to his feet and steered him to the doorway.

Tito stood framed in the opening, staring within. He stepped back to give them way. Greta Henry saw his heavy limp as he moved. Abandoning Neville to Quelí, she ran out to him. When Neville and Quelí emerged she had Tito backed against the external wall of the *jacal*, swiftly and soundlessly stripping at his clothing to uncover his wounds. He gently dissuaded her.

"Time enough, directly," he said. "Dinged a bit is all. Couple leaks that need a mite of plugging. Neville's got one, too, by the look of his shirt. Luck of the Stantons and I doubt we earned it. You all right, *querida?*"

Greta nodded and glanced at Quelí.

"Now," she agreed. "Both of us."

She leaned her cheek against his shoulder in gratitude.

"Enough to ask," Tito murmured. He looked at Neville, indicating the interior of the *jacal.* "Done?"

Neville nodded.

"Here, too," Tito said.

For the first time Neville became aware that all firing had ceased. There was no sign of further resistance within the enclosure. His arm clamped tighter on the packet and pouch beneath it.

"When I've made amends," he added.

Tito looked at him with unreadable eyes.

"Man could say you've done enough."

"Not yet," Neville said. "I never meant it to come to this." A surge of loyalty that had not been destroyed by Ted Crane's bullets gripped him. "Or Blair, either. Not at first, anyway."

Tito's lips set in a hard line.

"That I doubt to beat hell—about him," he said with harsh conviction. "But let be. You've made your peace with me. Now it's up to them coming yonder. We cut it close, *amigo*—"

He nodded toward the thin ribbons of grass twisting off to the north into the *malpaís*. Greta and Quelí followed the direction of his gesture and brightened eagerly. Neville turned with them. A compact body of hard-riding horsemen was pouring out between two tongues of the forbidding black lava at about a quarter mile's distance.

Neville had no difficulty singling out the figure of his father and those of Jaime Henry and the powerful, bareheaded black man who had taken their horses in the yard the night he and Blair had first ridden onto the Corona. They rode in the lead.

Two women were among the others. He supposed one to be the Indian tracker, Raúl Archuleta's daughter-in-law. The other, he saw with surprise and quick pleasure, was Rosa Martinez.

They swept on without slackening pace. Without order or signal they spread out in a wide line abreast in military fashion as the grass opened before them, making a furious, deadly charge. They clearly expected fire and were prepared to ride it down. It was not until their horses hurdled the wall in unison with almost drill-team precision that they could see the reason there was no defense and understand why they were not challenged.

Breaking right and left as they came, two small groups swept in opposite directions around the inner circumference of the wall, flushing out survivors. Only three crawled from hiding, hands high, and one of them

was wounded. Neville marvelled. He had himself
dropped only one of the Johnny Blues.

"Damned if you didn't do it!" he murmured to Tito.

"Wouldn't have if you hadn't put your one shot in the
right place," his half brother answered quietly. "I misfig-
ured and the bastard had me cold."

There was no time for further words. There was no
need.

The rest of the Corona crew came on to the *jacal* and
pulled up before it. Only one rider swung down. It was
Rosa Martinez. Before these people, without shyness,
she ran to Neville. She saw the blood below the
shoulder-yoke of his shirt and winced.

. "You're hurt!" she cried.

"Seemed like," he agreed. "Doesn't now."

She smiled and clung to the arm with the hook, oblivious to the blood upon it. All eyes swung to Spencer
Stanton. He sat motionless in his saddle. Jaime Henry
sat likewise beside him. Neither wasted time with questions for which their eyes could read the answers. Tito
and Quelí and Greta and Neville had survived. For
now that was enough. Spence Stanton's eyes set hard on
Neville.

"Your brother and the son of a bitch who was with
him when they killed Raúl Archuleta and jumped the
girls—Rosa showed us the place."

Tito answered for Neville, indicating the interior of
the *jacal*.

"In there. *Muerte, patrón.* Both. Crane killed Blair.
Neville killed Crane and rescued the girls."

"Bien," Stanton said. "The two of you, eh? To keep
our fat out of the fire. Wish I'd seen it. Brothers, by god,
when the chips were down! That's more like."

"No," Tito said. "No more'n half brothers. Ever.
Blood won't allow. But we damned well sweat together.
Call us *compañeros.* I sure as hell would if I had my
druthers."

"Companions?" Stanton snorted. "Comrades? Weak
words, after all this."

"Strong feelings," Tito answered.

Stanton's hawk eyes leaped to Neville.

"I warned you what would happen if you ever showed your face on the Corona again."

"Yes, sir," Neville said quietly. "I aim to pay the chit."

He tried to ease the packet and pouch from beneath his clamping arm. Sensing his intent, Rosa Martinez took them for him. She passed them up to Stanton.

This was the ultimate confrontation Neville had feared. It had not come about as he had planned but now that it was here the fear was gone. All that remained was a deep feeling of relief that he had survived for this moment. For that he was indebted to Tito Stanton.

"I stole six thousand dollars from your partner in the bank at Santa Fe," he told his father. "*I* did, on my own, without even Blair's knowledge until it was done. A loan, I told Saul Wetzel. I'm repaying it now. That packet contains what Blair and I bought with part of it. The rest is in that pouch."

Stanton balanced the pouch with Crane's two thousand dollars in it across one thigh and opened the oilskin packet. He studied the map and the documents within and then replaced them. The pouch of gold coins he thrust unopened into his own shirt.

"The gold's mine," he said. "It was gold you stole. It's gold you'll repay the rest with to the last penny, with interest. But the land's yours, for whatever this damned *malpaís* is worth. It was a shrewd idea and my own fault that I didn't plug this hole out here years ago. I'll not hold you or any other man to account for my own mistakes."

"And I'll not profit from mine," Neville answered. "If it goes a way to even the score, I'll be satisfied. Not for you. For Tito and Quelí. For the Stantons. All of them. For Rosa and Greta Henry and the family of the Corona man who was killed. For the Corona itself when it comes to that. The least I can do."

"For what?" Spencer Stanton demanded harshly. "No man gives up everything for nothing."

Neville glanced at Rosa Martinez. She smiled at him. He looked up at his father with a smile on his lips as well.

"An end to long riding," he said. "I lost my self-respect out here. I'd admire a chance to find it again."

Stanton retied the packet of papers from Santa Fe and thrust it also into his shirt. He rose in his stirrups.

"What the hell kind of womenfolk we raising in this country these days?" he demanded of Quelí and Greta Henry and Rosa Martinez. "We got two good hands need patching that were ventilated in line of duty. Goddamn it, that's Stanton blood they're wasting!"

DELL'S ACTION-PACKED WESTERNS

Selected Titles

- [ ] AUSTIN DAVIS by Wilson Young .... $ .95 (4430-02)
- [ ] BUCKAROO'S CODE by Wayne D. Overholser $ .95 (1422-08)
- [ ] BUCKSKIN MAN by Tom W. Blackburn .... $ 1.25 (0976-00)
- [ ] DRAW OR DRAG by Wayne D. Overholser . $ .95 (3263-06)
- [ ] EL SEGUNDO by Tom W. Blackburn ...... $ .95 (3491-00)
- [ ] FABULOUS GUNMAN
  by Wayne D. Overholser .... $ 1.25 (3191-03)
- [ ] GUNLOCK by Wayne D. Overholser ...... $ .95 (3322-13)
- [ ] THE GUNS OF DURANGO by Lou Cameron . $ .95 (4694-11)
- [ ] THE HILO COUNTRY by Max Evans .... $ .95 (3539-04)
- [ ] JEREMIAH PAINTER by George Wolk ..... $ .95 (4195-23)
- [ ] KING COLT by Luke Short .... $ .95 (4686-03)
- [ ] PATRON by Tom W. Blackburn .... $ .95 (4969-01)
- [ ] SHADOW MOUNTAIN by Bliss Lomax ..... $ .75 (7776-15)
- [ ] THE TRUTH ABOUT THE CANNONBALL KID
  by Lee Hoffman .... $ .95 (6140-08)
- [ ] THE VENGEANCE TRAIL OF JOSEY WALES
  by Forrest Carter $1.50 (9344-14)
- [ ] WEST OF THE RIMROCK
  by Wayne D. Overholser .... $ .75 (9586-03)
- [ ] WILEY'S MOVE by Lee Hoffman .... $ .95 (9822-07)

IT BEGAN WITH JUST
AN ORDINARY LITTLE DOG.

RABID

by David Anne

John and Paula had thought they had
found the perfect way to end their
holiday in France. They had had fun
outwitting the authorities by
smuggling a dog into England. And Asp
was a beautiful, loving corgi with
soft fur and limpid eyes. But the
horrible virus she concealed paralyzed
first a town, then the nation with fear.
As the disease mutated and became
airbone, it lashed out to terrorize the
entire world!

A DELL BOOK $1.95

Dell Bestsellers

- [ ] **ROOTS** by Alex Haley $2.75 (17464-3)
- [ ] **CLOSE ENCOUNTERS OF THE THIRD KIND**
  by Steven Spielberg $1.95 (11433-0)
- [ ] **THE CHOIRBOYS** by Joseph Wambaugh ... $2.25 (11188-9)
- [ ] **WITH A VENGEANCE** by Gerald Di Pego .. $1.95 (19517-9)
- [ ] **THIN AIR** by George E. Simpson
  and Neal R. Burger. $1.95 (18709-5)
- [ ] **BLOOD AND MONEY** by Thomas Thompson . $2.50 (10679-6)
- [ ] **PROUD BLOOD** by Joy Carroll $1.95 (11562-0)
- [ ] **NOW AND FOREVER** by Danielle Steel $1.95 (11743-7)
- [ ] **SNOWMAN** by Norman Bogner $1.95 (18152-6)
- [ ] **IT DIDN'T START WITH WATERGATE**
  by Victor Lasky $2.25 (14400-0)
- [ ] **DEATH SQUAD** by Herbert Kastle $1.95 (13659-8)
- [ ] **RABID** by David Anne $1.95 (17460-0)
- [ ] **THE SECOND COMING OF LUCAS BROKAW**
  by Matthew Braun $1.95 (18091-0)
- [ ] **HIDE IN PLAIN SIGHT** by Leslie Waller $1.95 (13603-2)
- [ ] **THE HIT TEAM** by David B. Tinnin
  with Dag Christensen $1.95 (13644-X)
- [ ] **EYES** by Felice Picano $1.95 (12427-1)
- [ ] **MAGIC** by William Goldman $1.95 (15141-4)
- [ ] **THE USERS** by Joyce Haber $2.25 (19264-1)
- [ ] **A GOD AGAINST THE GODS** by Allen Drury $1.95 (12968-0)
- [ ] **RETURN TO THEBES** by Allen Drury $1.95 (17296-9)
- [ ] **THE HITE REPORT** by Shere Hite $2.75 (13690-3)
- [ ] **THE OTHER SIDE OF MIDNIGHT**
  by Sidney Sheldon $1.95 (16067-7)
- [ ] **A DEATH IN CANAAN** by Joan Barthel ... $1.95 (11939-1)
- [ ] **UNTIL THE COLORS FADE** by Tim Jeal $2.25 (19260-9)
- [ ] **LOVE'S WILDEST FIRES** by Christina Savage . $1.95 (12895-1)
- [ ] **SUFFER THE CHILDREN** by John Saul $1.95 (18293-X)

At your local bookstore or use this handy coupon for ordering:

Dell **DELL BOOKS**
P.O. BOX 1000, PINEBROOK, N.J. 07058

Please send me the books I have checked above. I am enclosing $_____
(please add 35¢ per copy to cover postage and handling). Send check or money
order—no cash or C.O.D.'s. Please allow up to 8 weeks for shipment.

Mr/Mrs/Miss_____

Address_____

City_____ State/Zip_____

"WE ONLY HAVE ONE TEXAS"

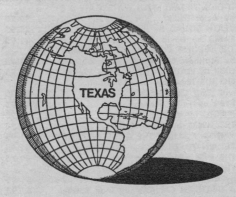

TEXAS

People ask if there is really an energy crisis. Look at it this way. World oil consumption is 60 million barrels per day and is growing 5 percent each year. This means the world must find three million barrels of new oil production each day. Three million barrels per day is the amount of oil produced in Texas as its peak was 5 years ago. The problem is that it is not going to be easy to find a Texas-sized new oil supply every year, year after year. In just a few years, it may be impossible to balance demand and supply of oil unless we start conserving oil today. So next time someone asks: "is there really an energy crisis?" Tell them: "yes, we only have one Texas."

ENERGY CONSERVATION - IT'S YOUR CHANCE TO SAVE, AMERICA

Department of Energy, Washington, D.C.